Under the Rising Moon

RASPBERRY RIDGE
BOOK TWO

JESSIE GUSSMAN

Contents

Acknowledgments

Cover art by Julia Gussman
Editing by Heather Hayden
Narration by Jay Dyess
Author Services by CE Author Assistant

Listen to the unabridged audio for FREE performed by Jay Dyess on the Say with Jay channel on YouTube. Get early access to all of Jay's recordings and listen to Jessie's books before they're available to the general public, plus get daily Bible readings by Jay and bonus scenes by becoming a Say with Jay channel member.

One

"Please stop."

Skyler Montgomery held one hand over her protruding belly, massaging the spot on the top left that always seemed to ache. Maybe the baby's head was pushing against her skin there.

"We just stopped. What's wrong with you?" Jeff Lewis, her boyfriend, er, fiancé, and the father of her baby, gave her a derisive look.

She felt like she was really putting him out by asking him to stop. "I'm pregnant. That's what's wrong. Your child is sitting on my bladder."

She tried to keep her voice modulated and not sound as annoyed as she felt. It wasn't her fault she had to pee. Was she supposed to pretend that she didn't? Suffer in silence? It wasn't like she demanded that he stop. She'd asked nicely.

The exit flew by, and she gritted her teeth.

"I really need to go. You're going to have to stop at the next exit, or you're going to have a mess on your nice pickup seat to clean up."

It wasn't an idle threat. She felt like she couldn't wait any longer. She'd tried to wait as long as she could before she said something, because she knew his reaction was going to be the way it was. That's the way it had been the last three times she'd asked to stop.

It wasn't like she was going every fifteen minutes. It had been two hours since they stopped before.

"You're more of a pain in the butt than you're worth," he mumbled to himself. "If you pee on my pickup seat, you're going to regret it."

He'd never exactly threatened her, but there were times, like now, that he made her feel like his possessions were more important than she was.

"Please. Let's don't fight. This is our last time together as a couple before the baby comes."

She was due in two weeks. And she had felt like she and Jeff were drifting apart. She knew she shouldn't have slept with him to begin with, not without a ring, a golden band, not the tiny engagement stone he'd given her, even if it had been a bit snug and she no longer wore it because her fingers had swelled with her pregnancy. But he'd been very persuasive, and she hadn't wanted him to get mad at her.

Plus, an engagement was almost like being married. They were committed to each other. There was nothing that could break their bond.

Anyway, she felt like they were drifting apart and had asked him to take a long weekend to spend it with her. She wanted to renew their spark because when the baby arrived, she'd been told that she'd be very busy, and sometimes relationships suffered in the newborn stage.

Hopefully her baby would be a good one, would sleep through the night, and would hardly ever cry.

It would be the first thing in her life that was easy, but she kinda felt like God owed her something easy, after all the hard things she'd gone through. She could hear her grandma saying that God didn't owe anyone anything, but she pushed those thoughts aside and set her jaw stubbornly. She could also hear her gram saying that she was too stubborn for her own good, then her Aunt Ruth, Gram's sister, would say, "Oh, Roberta, she's determined. She has perseverance; she's not stubborn."

Aunt Ruth always did see the best in her. Even more than her gram did. But that wasn't really saying much. Plus, both of those ladies had passed on years ago.

"If you don't want to fight, you shouldn't have started one. You threatened to pee on my seat. What are you, two?" Jeff spit the words out, sounding like the jerk her best friend always said he was.

After Kylie had OD'd, she hadn't had anyone else that she could call best friend. Unless she wanted to count Jeff. She wanted him to be her best friend. She heard that married couples should be each other's best friends, but Jeff wasn't exactly kind and compassionate the way Kylie was.

'Course, Kylie had gotten hooked on drugs, and toward the end, the only thing she cared about was making money so she could buy her next fix. So yeah, she'd stolen Skyler's stash that she had under her mattress from working at the diner outside of Chicago.

She could hardly be mad at Kylie, since shortly after she'd stolen the money and Skyler had figured it out and confronted her with that, Kylie had OD'd. And she was planning Kylie's funeral, not that it was much of a funeral.

She had never known how expensive it was to bury someone. Actually, it was cheaper to be cremated, so...she wasn't sure what Kylie's wishes were, but her friend had been cremated because that had been all Skyler could afford.

They'd had a little ceremony at the funeral home, although it was just Skyler and a couple other people from the diner who came.

She didn't know where Kylie's family was. Kylie never talked about them.

Kind of the way Skyler didn't really talk about her family either.

But she was going to turn over a new leaf and have a different life for her baby. Jeff was a respectable man with a steady job at Thompson's Trash and Recycling. He got up every morning at four o'clock and rode the garbage truck route around Chicago.

It was a hard job, but it paid well, and Jeff was a very dependable employee.

Of course, when he got off work on Friday afternoon, he was pretty much drunk from two hours later until the early hours of Sunday morning, but that's probably what she would do too if she had such a strenuous, difficult job.

"I won't pee on your seat. But I really do have to go. Please?"

"Fine. Whatever the next exit is, we'll take it. That's where you'll pee. Although, if you want to, I can stop along the road."

"No! I couldn't possibly go to the bathroom along the road. Someone might see me."

"It's not like they care. You're as big as a whale."

"That's why I need to pee all the time."

Jeff used to tell her she was the most gorgeous woman in the world. After a couple of beers, he acted like she was too.

Tears pricked her eyes, and she swallowed hard to push them away. Normal people were as big as a whale when they were pregnant. She was normal. And it wasn't completely abnormal for the father of the baby to look at a mother's pregnant body and not think she was sexy anymore.

Of course, she didn't really know how men thought, but they seemed to be attracted to the skinny girls. She'd always been skinny.

And she would be again, once the baby was born.

Lord, please let the next exit be soon. I don't think I can hold it too much longer.

She gritted her teeth against the pain as the baby moved and seemed to use her bladder as a trampoline, like it didn't already hurt the way it was lying on her.

If you were here, little guy, I would teach you where you're not allowed to sit, and that's on Mom's bladder.

She was going to teach her child everything she had been taught. Maybe she'd even take him to church. Gram had taken her once in a while, but by the time she'd gone to live at her grandma's house, she had been too big to think that there was much use in church. Then her gram had decided she was too old to deal with the stress and she'd gone into the system. Her gram had passed away not long after.

At least she'd gone to school. She had her high school diploma. That was more than Kylie had. Still, because of Skyler's good recommendation, the diner had hired Kylie. Or maybe it was just a shortage of workers. Seemed like they were always short-staffed and she was having to pick up extra shifts, especially on the weekend, which made Jeff mad.

She wasn't sure what she was going to do when the baby was born. She didn't have maternity leave, so she'd have to take off, but she wouldn't be paid for it. And they depended on her salary to buy groceries, especially Jeff's alcohol. It took everything he made to pay the rent on their small apartment.

"Have you thought about names?" she asked and then cringed. She shouldn't have, because Jeff got upset when she talked about the baby.

"I don't care what you name the stupid rug rat." He gave her a look that made her want to crawl into herself. "I wasn't the one who got knocked up to begin with."

She didn't say anything. She'd tried to explain to him that she'd taken her birth control pills exactly the way she was supposed to, and she hadn't missed even one. But he hadn't believed her. He said that never happened with any of his other girlfriends, and he acted like she betrayed him somehow. Like she'd chosen to get pregnant.

Of course, she didn't really mind that she was, because she had a baby to give all of her love to. And someone to love her as well.

She'd never really had that.

"And I'm looking forward to having some time together so we can work on our relationship."

"Our relationship doesn't need any work. At least not on my end. You need to shove that brat out and get your figure back. That's the only thing that's wrong with our relationship."

"Oh, I'm sure it won't take any time at all to get back into shape." She tried to project confidence, although she'd heard that some people had a lot of trouble getting back into shape. "When you talk like that, it makes me feel like you're only interested in my body. And that you don't really care about me as a person or about my emotions—"

"I care about your emotions. Just not when you're a whiny, complaining mess. No one could put up with that kind of crap the way I have."

It was true, she had been more emotional when she was pregnant.

"Oh my goodness. My back hurts so bad." She put a hand behind her back, at the spot where it felt like her muscles were being torn apart.

"See what I mean? All you ever do is complain. 'I have to pee. My back hurts.'" He mimicked her voice in a whiny tone. "When are you going to grow up?"

"And why don't you grow a little compassion? You don't need to be a jerk all the time. You don't have a human growing inside of your body, jumping on top of your bladder, making every muscle in your body ache, and then your boyfriend has to go and be in a grumpy mood all the time and complain because I don't look the way I did when we first started dating. You were there too. I didn't make this baby on my own."

It felt good to yell at him. She always tried to get along, and she hardly ever gave him a piece of her mind until she just couldn't hold it in anymore. He had been a jerk the whole trip, like he didn't really want to get away. It was true, they really couldn't afford it, but who knew when they would ever have a chance to do it again. She... She wanted a honeymoon. Something romantic and sweet. Where Jeff smiled and treated her like a queen and she did everything in her power to make his life happier and easier and they lived together and grew old together, but they needed couple time in order to grow that strong bond.

"If you yell at me, I'm not stopping for you. So I guess if you want to pee, you'd better be nice. There you go with your whining, bawling, and complaining all the time. I'm never good enough. If I'm not good enough, go find some other sugar daddy to suck from."

Her hand squeezed into a fist, but she tried to force herself to relax and open it back up. He didn't mean it. He was tired and grumpy. They'd been on the road for several hours since breakfast, and in order to save money, they agreed they weren't going to stop for fast food but would stop at a grocery store and grab some groceries before they camped out along Lake Michigan.

She swallowed, feeling the desire to cry again, and pushed it back. She could handle this. She could be nice, even when he was mean. She did remember that much from Sunday school. It was supposed to magically make everyone love her. She wanted Jeff to love her.

"I'm sorry. I love you, Jeff." She looked over, trying to give him a tremulous smile, but he just stared at her.

"If you loved me, you wouldn't be such a witch all the time."

She wanted to give him a piece of her mind, but instead, she said, "You're right. I'll try to be nice and try not to complain anymore."

"It's too late to stop. And your apology isn't good enough. You're gonna have to show me how sorry you are."

A sign that said "Raspberry Ridge - two miles" flew by as Jeff angrily grasped the wheel, speeding up like they weren't already going fifteen miles an hour over the speed limit.

Everything would be okay. They'd stop. He'd grab something to eat. They'd be fine. He wouldn't be grumpy anymore, and she wouldn't have to pee for at least another hour or two.

She wouldn't drink anything. That would help. She hadn't been drinking anything, though. Maybe she was a little dehydrated, because she had a headache. It had started thumping behind her eyes, and now it crisscrossed her forehead.

She didn't say anything when he jerked the wheel, hitting the exit at highway speed, and didn't start braking until they were almost at the stop sign.

Two

Jeff followed the narrow road toward Raspberry Ridge, and Skyler assumed that he thought there was probably a gas station there.

But she hadn't seen any of those signs that said that there was gas or even food in Raspberry Ridge. It was probably one of those tiny little towns that didn't even have a stoplight.

They were foreign to her, living in the Chicago suburbs the way she had. But they were quaint too, and every once in a while, she'd see something on TV that made her think that maybe living in one of those little towns wouldn't be too bad. Yeah, it'd be inconvenient to not be able to walk to work, since the diner was only a block away from where they lived, or walk to get groceries either, since the grocery store was just two blocks down the street. She didn't need a car, which was good, because she couldn't afford the expense.

They drove by a few houses, and there was one small, tiny store. They went by before Jeff must have realized that there wasn't anything else.

"All right. There you go. Go pee," he said as he came to a stop, at least a block down from the store they passed.

There was nothing but a few older-looking houses, rather unkept and spaced far apart at this end of the street.

"Go on. Get out!" he said in a louder, commanding tone that she didn't argue with.

She wasn't even sure the store up the street had a bathroom, but if it didn't, maybe she could go behind one of the houses that looked like they were abandoned and take care of things.

She didn't want to do that, but she couldn't get back in the truck without going. She really was going to pee herself if she didn't get some relief soon.

"Do you want anything?" she asked, hating the way her voice sounded small and timid.

"Freedom," Jeff muttered.

She pretended she didn't hear, straightened up, and slammed the door shut. She realized as she was closing it that she left her purse on the seat.

Well, she could hardly buy him anything if she didn't have her purse, and maybe that would be just as well. She didn't exactly have money to spend anyway.

Debating for two seconds about whether to open the door and grab her purse or not, she finally decided that she wouldn't. Maybe he'd see it and come in. If he brought her purse to her, it would be the one nice thing he did for her that day.

Feeling like she was waddling rather than walking, she turned and made her way up the sidewalk. She couldn't imagine having a child to take care of and being pregnant at the same time. How did other women do it? She was so miserable she could hardly stand it. She couldn't imagine having more than Jeff to deal with.

He was just about as bad as a little kid.

She walked up to the store, and the bell rang as she opened it. Cheerful and friendly, the exact opposite of her mood. But she never stayed down long, and the tinkling bell made her smile with its dulcet tones and old-fashioned welcome. Like something she might have seen on TV.

An older lady stood behind the counter, glasses on her head connected to a chain that went around her neck. They sat perched below her nose, and she looked over them as Skyler walked in.

"Hello, sweetheart," the old lady said. She lifted her nose a little bit as though smelling the air and that would give her a clue as to where Skyler had come from. "Can I help you with something? Or are you browsing today?"

"I might want to browse a little bit, but...I need to use the restroom. Do you have one?"

The lady paused for a moment, and then a little smile tilted up the corners of her mouth as her eyes dipped to Skyler's large, round belly, which preceded her everywhere she went, and then back up to Skyler's face, which was almost assuredly puffy and bloated-looking. Her entire body felt bloated.

"Typically, customers are not allowed in the back, but I'll make an exception for you," the lady said, and her eyes squinted as her face wreathed in a smile. It was a friendly, kind smile, which made Skyler feel welcome, like someone didn't mind her presence, when she'd felt like an imposition all day to Jeff.

"So, are you here to visit relatives?" the lady said, walking out from behind the counter as she waved a hand for Skyler to follow her down the hall.

"No. My boyfriend and I are taking a little time away before the baby comes. We need to work on our relationship. I want it to be strong, because I want my baby to have a better home than I did."

"I see," the woman said, and there was no censure in her voice. Although Skyler realized she should have said fiancé. She wanted to correct herself. Let the lady know that she wasn't just someone shacking up with her boyfriend, but she had an actual promise in hand.

Not that everyone she knew didn't live together before they got married. She didn't know a couple who didn't. That was how a person practiced for marriage, wasn't it?

She wasn't quite sure about that. It felt a little bit like they were practicing to not get married, since there was no commitment between them. And it felt like Jeff's hand hovered over the eject button, ready to push it at any time.

Maybe it was just her. Maybe it worked out for other people.

"You can go here. And you came just in time. I'm not usually open, but I had some bookwork to do, and I figured I'd flip the sign while I did it. I wasn't expecting to get any customers, so you were a pleasant surprise."

"Nice. I like being a pleasant surprise."

She couldn't remember the last time anybody had told her she was a pleasant anything. Although Kylie had said she was a good friend. After she'd stolen the money, Skyler had said that they could still be friends, even though she hoped Kylie was going to pay it back.

That was her nest egg, in case things didn't work out with Jeff. She didn't think that a person should have a contingency. When they made a commitment to a relationship, they should remain committed. But something in her bones just told her that Jeff wasn't the kind of person who was going to stick around.

Plus, he hurt her so often with his nasty comments about her figure and made her feel like the only thing he wanted was her body. It...made her feel like one body was probably just as good as another. But he didn't really like her. The part of her that made up who she was.

Regardless, she thanked the lady.

"How long do you think you're going to browse after you're done here?"

"Probably not long. My boyfriend is waiting. But your store looks really cute."

She meant that. There were lots of little things hanging around, things that she would love to use to decorate her apartment with. But she didn't really have any money to purchase anything.

Maybe if Kylie hadn't taken all of her money, she'd take a little bit of her stash and buy a few trinkets for the baby's room. She hadn't bought a crib yet, since it cost three weeks' paychecks, and she wasn't sure what she was going to do.

Kylie said she was going to plan a baby shower, but that was before she OD'd.

Anyway, she heard babies grew really fast anyway, and she probably would need to buy bigger clothes for him sooner than she thought. So she didn't want to get too many clothes that were too small.

Although she loved going in the store and just fingering them. They were so cute.

The lady stood aside so Skyler could walk into the restroom. It was decorated the way the rest of the store was, with lots of trinkets hanging everywhere, rose-colored wallpaper, and an old-fashioned pedestal sink.

That was all the small space could hold. It was just a sink and a toilet, with a shelf over the back of the toilet with some more trinkets on it.

A big mirror over the sink told her that she had been right, her face was blotchy and puffy and she looked like she'd been crying. Even though she felt like she'd sucked all the tears back and hadn't let a single one come out.

"I'll be right here whenever you're done," the lady said, and Skyler had the door closed before she realized what the lady meant by that.

She didn't want to leave her back here by herself because she thought Skyler was going to steal something.

That made her mad. How could the lady look at her and assume she was a thief?

Of course she wasn't any such thing. How judgy could a person be?

But then, her Aunt Ruth had always told her to try to put herself in somebody else's shoes, and if she were in that lady's shoes, maybe she'd be worried about that too. After all, her very best friend in the world had stolen every cent that she had, and while Skyler knew that if Kylie had asked, Skyler would have given it to her, she still couldn't blame the lady for trying to protect what was hers. She would. Especially if it meant she was protecting her baby.

She would just like to see anyone try to come between her and her baby. She would fight like a wildcat to protect him.

It's a wonder she hadn't scratched Jeff's eyes out for calling her a brat.

Soon blessed relief came, although she had to contort herself to fit in the bathroom as she struggled to rearrange her clothes, since there wasn't nearly enough room for her bulky stomach.

Maybe even if she wasn't pregnant, it would be a tight squeeze, but being pregnant made it feel like she was a loaf of bread popping out of a sardine can.

She made sure to wash her hands well after she flushed the toilet, and she spent a second or two looking at her face, wondering if there was anything she could do.

She hadn't bought makeup for months, not since shortly after she found out she was pregnant. Once she did, she'd saved every penny she could for the things she knew she needed for the baby.

Maybe it would be easier if she had family.

Maybe if she lived in this town, this lady would be like family.

"Thank you, ma'am," she said as she came out of the restroom, her anger over the idea that the lady thought she was going to steal something fading away. It was funny how putting herself in someone else's shoes could do that. Sometimes she wasn't able to, like Jeff. She didn't understand how he could get off being so mean to her, when most of the time she tried as hard as she could to be nice.

That wasn't the way he treated her when they first started dating. But once they moved in together, it was like he treated her like she didn't matter anymore. That he had gotten her, and he didn't need to try to keep her.

That was mostly true. Her Aunt Ruth had told her that she should commit to a relationship. And when she committed, she should do everything she could to make that relationship the best it could be.

Aunt Ruth hadn't said what to do if the other person in the relationship wasn't doing the same thing.

"So, you're taking a trip?" the lady asked as she allowed Skyler to walk in front of her down the hallway to the store. "Are you heading to Lake Michigan for a day on the sand?"

"Yeah. We're actually going to camp out on the beach. But we're going a little further north. Up where it's not quite so populated." She wasn't sure it was exactly legal to do what Jeff had suggested—just camp on the beach somewhere.

"Oh. You want some privacy for the romance aspect," the woman said, and there was a smile in her voice.

"Yeah. Something like that," Skyler said. It was mostly because further north, they could camp on the shore without worrying about being kicked out by the local authorities. At least that's what they'd heard. Skyler had a bad feeling about it, but Jeff wouldn't listen to her...

She made it to the store, the scent of raspberry filling the room from a scented candle that was lit on the counter, and Skyler remembered the town was called Raspberry Ridge.

She hadn't seen the shore and couldn't recall seeing Lake Michigan in the distance, but she supposed they were pretty close. Regardless, she had told the lady that she was going to browse some, and she wanted to keep her word, so she didn't walk straight to the door.

Instead, she walked down the crowded aisle. Flip-flops were neatly stacked on one end, all sizes and colors, but only one style. Then there were beach towels folded neatly in a bin. She smiled at the umbrellas held in a bucket and looked longingly at the kites.

She'd never actually flown a kite, but she'd always wanted to. It looked like fun. Kites looked so cheerful and happy.

Maybe someday after her son got old enough, they could buy a kite and learn to fly it together. She could imagine them having a lot of fun on the shores of the lake. They could go to the lake in Chicago, although she'd need a car or to hire an Uber or something.

She could cross that bridge when she got to it. Maybe by then, she'd be able to afford a car.

She had to get a raise at the diner, and Jeff would need to get overtime at the waste management company, but he'd been talking about doing that a lot anyway. Mostly to get away from her.

Maybe if the baby cried, it would drive him out of the house, and he'd earn money for them. And she'd learn how to keep the baby from crying, and then they'd be happy.

"Just let me know if you need anything," the lady said, already settled back behind the counter. "I'll be another five minutes or so."

"All right. Thank you."

She had gotten to the end of the store and looked out the window. The streets were deserted, the town quiet.

This was definitely the smallest town she'd ever been in. She kind of liked it. Maybe if the lady behind the counter knew her, she would trust her to go to the bathroom by herself. After all, she wasn't the slightest bit tempted to steal any of the little onesies that had *Raspberry Ridge, a great place to grow up* on them. Even though they were super cute, and she had to agree with the sentiment. Even though she wouldn't be raising her son in Raspberry Ridge.

There were some bibs with big raspberries on them and a couple of little sailor outfits that were absolutely adorable.

She skimmed over the tiny dresses they had for the baby girls. She hadn't found out what she was having. She hadn't gone to many prenatal appointments. Although she had gone and gotten prenatal vitamins, and she took them almost every day.

But she knew she was having a boy. She just knew it. Like a mother's intuition. Her first mother's intuition, and it made her smile. She hoped to have lots more intuition about her son, since she imagined they would be extremely close as he grew up, and she would teach him how to treat women with respect and courtesy, opening their doors and stopping whenever they needed to use the restroom, not making them hold it until they felt like their back teeth were floating. Especially if they were pregnant with their baby.

She reached the door, and she had her hand on the knob before she turned. "Thanks for letting me use the restroom. I saw some things I'd really like to purchase. If I come back, maybe I will."

She wished she could have bought something as a goodwill gesture for the lady letting her use her private bathroom, but since she left her purse on the seat, she really couldn't.

The bell jingled again as she walked through it, the sound still making her smile. Maybe she should get bells like that to put above the door of the baby's room so they jingled and would make him smile every time his mom walked in.

She was still smiling about that when she looked up the street and then down, then back up.

She blinked, shielded her eyes from the sun, and looked again.

It was still deserted. Completely and totally deserted.

There wasn't a single car parked along the street, which, when they drove in, there wasn't either. It seemed like everyone parked off the street in this neck of the woods. Which wasn't unheard of in Chicago. In fact, there were whole communities like that. Rich communities. People who could afford enough real estate not only for a house but also to park their car. A luxury.

But here, buildings weren't side by side or stacked on top of each other, and there was plenty of room, so it made sense there were no cars parked along the street, except there should have been one.

A red pickup. There should have been a red pickup along the street, somewhere.

But she looked down the flat Michigan street and saw nothing. It ended at a gate with a sign hanging on it. One she couldn't read, and over the gate, there was some scrub brush growing, but over the scrub brush, she could see the sparkling water of Lake Michigan and the blue sky above, and she couldn't quite make out the line where they met.

She looked back the other direction, and the flat road went straight off into the horizon.

No cars.

Nothing.

Three

Homer Aiken stared at his computer screen. He had been working since before the sun was up on his latest computer program, and he'd just found a solution to an issue that he'd run into and been working on for the last hour and a half.

If he looked away and squinted into the corner of the room, looking deep into his head, he could almost see it. He squinted a little more, as though the clearer he could see the wall, the clearer things would appear in his brain.

A crash made him jump in his seat, and he put a hand on the desk, making a loud smack.

Everything that had been in his brain vanished, the solution, the numerals he needed, everything.

Tempted to ignore the sound and turn back to his computer, he knew he couldn't.

His mother had been getting steadily worse. When she had first been diagnosed, it hadn't been bad.

He'd been able to continue to work from home just fine. Most people needed the company of other humans and enjoyed working in the city, even though each day was more of the same. He didn't mind the solitude; he actually appreciated it, since he didn't enjoy going into the office every day, didn't like the bright lights or the crowd of people around him. He much preferred being alone. An introvert was what they called him, and he supposed it was true. He could live without seeing people ever.

He could hear his mother mumbling, although he couldn't hear the words she said, and he pushed back away from his desk with one last look at his screen before hurrying to the door of his study. His walls were lined with bookshelves, most of them put back correctly, although most of them were his mother's religious tomes. Ones he had read at one time or another but hadn't picked up in a while.

"Mom?" he said as he stepped out of his study door, closing the door behind him.

"Mom? Are you okay?" His voice echoed down the wide hallway. At one time, the house they lived in was considered quite a modern mansion, with big rooms, wide hallways, and high ceilings. Built at the beginning of the twentieth century, it was made out of brick, which was a huge luxury at the time. The brick had been painted a cheerful yellow during his childhood, although it had faded to a happy cream in the years since.

He supposed he should take some of his moldy money and paint the house.

But he didn't want to take any of his moldy money and put his mother in a home. She had made him promise that he would not do that to her, back when she still had full use of her faculties.

He had promised, thinking it wouldn't be that hard to take care of one old lady.

He also thought it would be a long time before he was in that position. But his mother had early-onset Alzheimer's, possibly brought on by the stress of his dad leaving years ago.

Homer had had the greatest admiration for his father, until he had left his mother.

If there was one thing Homer couldn't stand, it was a man who didn't stand up and do his duty. It didn't help that his dad had driven away with a long-legged, skinny woman in a miniskirt, thirty years younger than he was, approximately Homer's age, hanging onto his arm.

Homer was surprised she didn't have one hand in his wallet, and he might have said that.

His dad acted shocked that Homer would suggest such a thing, and the woman looked equally outraged. Or maybe her expression was smug.

He hadn't seen him since. That had been almost fifteen years ago when Homer was eighteen.

Now, his mom was in the latter stages or...at least what he had read about the latter stages. This disease could last for years. She could be completely gone, not know who she was or who anyone was, and yet, with a healthy heart and no cancer, she could live for...a long time.

He would never have thought that he would wish his mother to die, and he didn't now. Truly. But the idea of those long years, here in the house taking care of her, felt a little overwhelming.

One day at a time. One hour. One minute. One second sometimes was all he could do.

"Mom?" He had gone down the steps and had looked in the big, formal living room and glanced in the formal dining room as well. Now he checked the other side of the home and in the kitchen which originally had been smaller with a dining room off of the cooking area, but when his mother had remodeled when Homer had been a boy, she had made it all one big room. Huge windows, lots of sunlight, tons of cupboard space, and a nice big island in the middle. He remembered sitting on that island, eating chocolate chip cookies, and listening to the Old-fashioned Revival Hour quartet with Rudy Atwood at the piano on the radio.

He didn't know where his mom had found that station. None of his friends had ever listened to that kind of music.

Regardless, those were fond memories, and there she was, standing in the kitchen, her back to the stove. One burner red-hot, although there was nothing sitting on it, and the microwave running, although he couldn't see anything in that either.

He walked over and pushed the cancel button on the microwave before he shut the burner off. "Mom? What are you doing?"

"I can't find your father's galoshes. You know how he loves those things. And if I don't have them for him when he comes home from work, he won't take you out for your daily walk along the lake!"

"That would be terrible, wouldn't it?" he said, having learned a long time ago it was better to just play along with her as much as he could, rather than trying to correct her. He had no idea if his dad ever owned galoshes, and if he had, little Miss Hand-in-his-wallet would probably have taken them if she thought they could be sold for any kind of money. Not to mention, he and his dad hadn't taken their daily walk along the lake since he had started elementary school.

So that's what year she was in. He tried to remember.

"Are you getting together with Karen and Linda?" he asked, remembering the ladies who were in the prayer group that met on Wednesdays.

"Oh!" his mother said, her hand going to her hair as though trying to figure out whether she fixed it that day or not.

He could tell her she hadn't.

"I didn't know today was Wednesday. Why didn't you tell me?"

"I'm sorry. I must have forgotten to tell you."

He looked around the kitchen, seeing her decorative old-fashioned milk can had been knocked over. That must have been the cause of the crash he had heard. Thankfully, because who knew what she would have caught on fire with that burner going. And she'd broken a couple of microwaves by doing what she had just done. Either running them empty or putting some kind of metal in them.

Talk about a good explosion. He had watched the remote catch on fire. That was before the TV had died.

He wasn't quite sure what his mom thought she was warming up when she put the remote in, but she had broken the microwave over it.

There was a part of him that was fascinated over the chemistry behind the microwave and what it did to inorganic objects, but at the time, he had been split between thinking about that and realizing that his mom was seriously declining.

Maybe he should hire an in-home aid.

But he resisted that. He wanted his privacy. He didn't want to have someone in the house, nosing around in his business, getting involved in his work, interrupting his schedules, or trying to get him to do things he didn't want to.

He worked best when he knew exactly what time things were going to happen, but sometimes he had inspiration in the middle of the night, and that's when he got up and worked. Then, he would take a nap during the day. Lately, if he napped during the day, it had to be on the couch and with one eye open. Because he had to watch his mother.

"Wait. It's been years since Linda and Karen and I met for prayer group. What are you trying to do, Homer? Confuse this old lady?"

That sounded like his mom.

"Mom. No. Sorry. I... I guess I got a little confused." He cleared his throat a bit and put a hand behind his neck. He didn't want to lie to her. Didn't believe in lying. She definitely raised him to know lying was a sin. Just like not keeping your vows.

Take that, Dad.

Still, he just tried to go with the flow. Unable to keep up with her changing reality. The science behind that was fascinating as well. What caused the brain to one minute be here, one minute be in 1982?

He had no idea.

It was interesting to think about. Surely they could find a cure for that. He'd heard that a person was what they ate, but his mom always ate healthy. She had home-cooked their meals every evening. And she had a huge vegetable garden outside since he was small, although the older he got, the more flowers she had, until he graduated from college and it was mostly all flowers and potatoes.

Maybe that was it. Too much meat and potatoes. They were too Irish. The Scots-Irish in him was what made him pinch pennies though, and he wasn't going to begrudge his ancestors their potatoes.

"What time do we eat lunch? Eleven? I can't seem to remember. What day is it?" his mom said, scrunching her brows up and looking around as though she normally fed him. Which was not true. Much to his disappointment. Although, it hadn't been hard to learn to cook. Cooking was easy. It wasn't rocket science. Rocket science was hard.

He ought to know.

Regardless, he'd learned to cook, partially from watching her. Once she realized that it was something he wanted to learn how to do, she told him how to make all of his favorite meals, most of which did include meat and potatoes.

"You had a hard day, Mom. It's no wonder you can't remember. How about you sit down, and I'll make us a couple of sandwiches for lunch?"

He wasn't sure what he was going to do when she couldn't feed herself. Couldn't...use the restroom on her own.

They'd had a couple of accidents, which he'd been able to get cleaned up without too much embarrassment on his end. Thankfully, she was in one of her times where she didn't recognize him, and it wasn't too bad. She didn't remember either episode, anyway, which was just fine by him.

Growing up, if someone had told him that he would be cleaning up his mother's messes, at least in that regard, he probably would have moved to a different continent.

The fact that he was still there and was facing the potential that he would do that very thing someday and soon said, to him at least, that he had matured a little from that time in his life.

His mom sat down at the bar, which was an indication that she really wasn't herself. His mom, as he knew her as he was growing up, never sat down in her kitchen and allowed someone else to work in it while she watched.

So that was a clue.

But he went to the big stainless steel fridge and pulled out the leftover chicken that he made the night before.

His mom didn't typically use soda in her meals, but he found this recipe online and really loved it. It took Dr Pepper, which was not his favorite kind of soda, but it was a little sweeter than some of the others and had a taste that went well with the chicken.

It had turned into one of their favorite meals, and he loved the leftovers as well.

After making a sandwich, sticking some lettuce and onion and tomato on it, just to pretend that he was making it healthy, he stuck it in the microwave for a few seconds to take the chill off.

Meanwhile his mother chattered, and from what she was saying, he could tell that her one moment of lucidity had faded, and now she was back…maybe fifteen years ago. Before his dad left.

Interesting that most of her memories were from before he left. Maybe it was because her memories had gone downhill since then.

Another thing he blamed his dad for. He thought maybe his mom wouldn't have gotten so bad so fast if his dad had stuck around. It was really hard not to feel bitter and angry and feel like his dad was a lily-livered pansy for not manning up and taking care of the woman he pledged his life to.

Of course, Homer wasn't married and most likely never would be, so it was kind of rude for him to judge. He'd never walked in his dad's shoes.

"Here you go, Mom. You didn't know your kid could cook, did you?"

"My kid? I have a kid?" She looked around like she was expecting to see an eight-year-old running into the kitchen.

"That's me, Mom. I'm your kid."

Her eyes opened wide. "I thought you were my husband. Are you married?"

He'd pretended to be his dad so many times it wasn't even funny. Nothing weird, just he must look like his dad. Because his mom got them confused a lot.

"I guess we are. I'm glad you reminded me," he said easily, and then he said, "Do you want to pray for us?"

She never forgot how to pray. She didn't forget how to sing either. She could recite Bible verses even if she thought the year was 1990, and she could sing every single verse of every hymn he'd ever heard and some that he hadn't.

She always talked to God, she never forgot that He was her Heavenly Father, that He loved her, and that she was saved by the blood of Jesus.

He would have wondered about that, if she had. He believed that once a person was saved, they were always saved, the Bible was clear about that, that nothing could pluck you out of God's hand, but couldn't a person make a choice to jump?

The Bible didn't answer the question, and it wasn't one that he had seen theologians discuss. There were just two sides. The side who believed you could lose your salvation, and the side who believed you couldn't.

He supposed he had a foot mostly on the side that believed you couldn't, but he did, maybe in the back of his mind, believe that a person could make a decision to reject what he had believed before and turn his back on Jesus.

He didn't think that God would hold his mother accountable if she were to do that in her mental state, but he supposed it was something that he wouldn't have thought of ten years ago, or even five, but sometimes when a person was a caregiver, they had a lot of time to think, and they thought about some crazy things.

That was one of his.

When they were done eating, his mother got up, taking their plates and putting them in the dishwasher, even though she still thought he was her husband.

"I believe I'm going to lie down for a little bit. What are you going to do, dear?"

"I think I'll go work. I'll be in my study if you need me."

"I'll be right here. You let me know when you're ready for supper. I'll... I think I have something started."

"You do," he assured her, even though it was him that had started supper in the crockpot.

The crockpot was an amazing invention, and he didn't know how people had lived without it.

He watched as his mother left the kitchen, walked over to the family room, sat down on the settee, and curled her legs up beside her as she laid her head on the pillow.

It wasn't nearly long enough for her to stretch out, but it was her favorite place to sleep. Maybe because it made her feel cocooned and warmed. He remembered her saying something like that a few years ago, back when they still had conversations. He got the feeling that since his dad had left, his mom had missed his presence beside her when they slept.

As for Homer, he kind of liked lying spread eagle out on his bed and had often wondered if he got married, which did not seem likely, where in the world his wife would sleep. He'd have to cramp his style a little, if she were going to sleep in the bed with him.

He hadn't spent a lot of time worrying about that. He had other things to think about.

And now that he got up and walked around a little, he could see the solution to the problem he'd been working on clearly in his mind.

He never liked being interrupted, but typically, it worked out for the best.

He could just hear his mom saying to let go and let the Lord work. Meaning, let go of his plans and his timeline and let God take control and do things in His own time.

She had a lot of wisdom.

He ascended the stairs slowly, trying not to think about everything she'd lost and, instead, trying to think a little more about what God wanted him to learn.

Patience, maybe. And maybe also that sometimes interruptions, while they seemed annoying at the time, could actually be beneficial.

Four

Jeff had left her.

That was all Skyler could think as she walked back down the sidewalk for the fifth time. She'd walked up and down and up and down until she actually had to go to the bathroom again. But the sign had long since been turned to "closed" on the one store in town, and there were no other stores.

Her stomach rumbled. She was starving. And to top everything off, she'd been having those annoying Braxton Hicks contractions for the last two hours.

They actually hurt worse than the other Braxton Hicks she'd been having since about the sixth month of her pregnancy.

The one time she'd gone to the ER, rushing because she thought she was in premature labor, the doctor had told her that it was common, and that if she had come to her appointments, she would know that.

She had felt called out. Yelled at like a schoolgirl. Like she had done something wrong by not going to her prenatal appointments.

They had all been the same. They just measured her, listened for the heartbeat, and made her pee in a cup.

They never did anything different, and they charged her fifty dollars every time she went. She didn't have any health insurance. Although, she had looked around and knew that she could get state health insurance for her baby. She planned to do that, and it would be free, unless Jeff made too much. And then, they'd have to pay something.

She didn't really like doing that, but she didn't have a choice. After looking into buying health insurance for herself and her child, she about fell off her chair. The monthly premium was more money than she made in a month. She couldn't pay the premium, let alone still have money to buy groceries or pay rent.

She had hoped that Jeff would help with those things, but he was careful to keep their finances separate, although he paid the rent. That was the biggest bill. But since he paid that, he expected her to buy everything else, including his alcohol.

Regardless, none of it mattered now. She had no idea what she was going to do, and she scolded herself for the hundredth time for leaving her purse on the seat. It had been selfish of her. She hadn't wanted to have to buy him anything, so she was going to use not having her purse as an excuse.

But her phone, her wallet, her driver's license, everything that she needed was in that little bag, and...it was now wherever Jeff was.

She didn't actually believe he was never coming back for her. He just wanted to teach her a lesson. Although what that lesson was, she wasn't sure.

Not to have to go to the bathroom? Good luck with that.

She stopped, bending over a little as her stomach squeezed.

Not to get pregnant? Yeah, well, he was there for that too. And from what she recalled, it was more him than her.

She tried to shove that thought aside. It wasn't very nice. But Jeff wasn't always the most considerate lover.

Actually, his consideration in that area had waned considerably when she moved in with him. His actions had often echoed his words, and she just felt like a body.

Nothing more.

She didn't know what other lesson he might want her to learn, other than maybe giving her a better idea that if she had a chance to pick out another guy, she'd make sure she picked out one who wasn't a jerk.

But she didn't want to think along those lines either. She didn't want to be the kind of person who left when things got hard. She wanted to be able to stick things out, do what she said she was going to do, make a commitment, and keep it.

Except, she wished she'd been a little smarter about who she made a commitment to.

Well, if she had another chance... She didn't want to think like that. She wanted to be faithful, and she wanted them to make their relationship work. But it was going to take both of them. Unless she could hold up everything by herself.

But she could hardly do that without her phone, her wallet, her bank card, not that there was that much money in her account, and a hundred miles away from her home!

Tears pricked her eyes, like they had been doing more and more lately and more and more that afternoon. It must have been the sixth or seventh time that she tried hard not to cry. And then she thought, *What does it matter? Who cares if I cry? Jeff isn't here to tell me I'm being a baby.*

But when he came back for her, she didn't want him to find her sitting by the side of the road, blubbering like the baby he always called her. She wanted him to find her poised, totally unconcerned, and having full confidence that he would return.

No, it was hard for her to keep the boiling anger down. She wanted to grab a hold of him and smack his head against something really, really hard.

Her stomach tightened, pain pushing through and down her hips. She stopped, bending over. That hurt. A lot. If these were just fake contractions, she couldn't imagine what real labor was like.

Jeff had wanted her to have the baby at home because he thought it would be cheaper. Thank goodness she hadn't gone for that. She couldn't imagine going through pain worse than this without painkillers or an epidural. They could put her to sleep and just take the baby. Except, she wanted to see him. She couldn't wait to. The thought made her smile.

Still, the sun was going down, and Jeff was probably going to show up soon.

But she needed a place to sit down. She'd been on her feet for hours, and maybe the Braxton Hicks contractions wouldn't hurt so much if she wasn't on her feet.

She passed a wooden house. It had been painted blue, a pretty, baby blue shade, like a blanket. Except, the two blankets she had for her baby were both brown. That's all the secondhand store had.

She came to the last house before the cliffs on that side of the road. A pretty creamy yellow brick with an old wrought iron fence that surrounded a tangle of weeds with flowers that struggled to push through. It might have been a garden at one time.

An older lady, younger than the lady in the store, but older than Skyler, worked in the garden.

As the cramp eased, she realized she had to go to the bathroom again, and this was the first person she'd seen all afternoon.

"Ma'am?" she asked as she stopped beside the wrought iron gate, her hand on it but not making a move to open it. She didn't want to look like she was going to trespass no matter what the lady said.

"Ma'am?" she called again, when the lady didn't answer. She realized she was humming to herself, something that sounded like a hymn. Something her grandmother might have sung back in the day.

"Hello! My goodness, Linda. I didn't see you there. Come on in."

Skyler looked behind her, then up and down the sidewalk. There was no one else in sight. She looked at the woman again, who was moving toward her, a pleased expression on her face like she was about to greet a friend.

"Um, I'm not Linda. But if you don't mind, I would appreciate it if you'd let me in any way. I have to go to the bathroom."

"Linda. Today's Bible study. And of course you can use our bathroom. You know that my bathroom is open for anyone in Bible study."

"I don't have a Bible, ma'am. And I can't have Bible study, because my boyfri—" She stopped abruptly. She had to stop doing that. "My *fiancé* will be here anytime."

"Linda. Our children are the same age, remember?"

"Um, mine's still in utero," she said, pointing to her belly.

"Linda! I didn't know you were expecting! Does Charles know?"

She wasn't sure who Charles was.

"You said I could use your restroom?" she said, feeling a little creeped out but knowing that she needed to take the opportunity to go, because who knew when she'd get to go again. When Jeff picked her up, he probably wasn't going to want to stop until they got wherever they were going. At the rate she was going, she kind of wished they could get a hotel. She was exhausted, tired of these stupid fake contractions that hurt like sixty, and just wanted to lie down for a little bit.

"Of course, Linda. We can talk about the baby later. If Charles doesn't know... You're going to have to tell him."

"Yeah. I will."

"You mean you haven't yet?" She made a kissing sound with her mouth. "I told you that having an affair was not a good idea."

"Yeah. Tell me about it," Skyler said under her breath. She'd seen too many relationships ruined because people couldn't stick together. She didn't know what was so hard about it. Sure, Jeff wasn't the easiest person to live with, but she certainly wasn't going to go mess around on him. And she was going to do her best to love him, even though he made it difficult at times. Back before she got pregnant, he was a lot nicer. Surely when she had the baby, he would turn back into that nice guy.

"Well, what do you expect? That's sad. But at least you gave Phil up... You did give Phil up, right? We talked about that, and you said you were going to tell him that you were married and couldn't do that anymore."

"Yeah. I gave him up," Skyler said, just going along with the woman. She had no idea who Charles was, or Phil, and the father of her baby definitely knew that he was going to be a father, so she had no one left to tell.

The woman smiled and opened the back door, leading Skyler into a beautifully modern hall, which Skyler would not have guessed with the way the exterior of the house looked. The floor was a creamy yellow tile, with black grout, and it went beautifully with the bluish gray walls. An expensive-looking light fixture hung from the ceiling, and the house was cool, calm, and welcoming.

"Here's the restroom. You know the layout of the house, and you can find the kitchen from here. I'll be waiting. We need to talk."

Skyler walked into the bathroom, spacious for a downstairs facility, and closed the door behind her.

A mirror on the wall was framed with dark wood, maybe walnut? Skyler wasn't sure. She didn't hang with the rich folk. That's what this house felt like. That it belonged to rich people. Except...the outside was rather shaky.

But the bathroom was well appointed, well lit, and she didn't feel squished, despite her huge belly.

Her contractions had not stopped, but they were ten or fifteen minutes apart, and she figured once she was able to sit down and maybe even put her feet up, although Jeff hated it when she put her feet up on his dash, they would probably completely go away.

But first she had to get out of this lady's house. Although...she wouldn't mind walking through. This was the nicest house she'd ever been in. The floors gleamed, and the pictures on the walls were interesting. The hall was spacious, and the rooms looked large, with heavy, ornate furniture and large, expensive-looking rugs. She'd even seen fireplaces.

What would it be like to live in a house like this?

The question was so ridiculous she laughed out loud, then stifled the sound.

She didn't want the lady to think she was crazy, although she was starting to feel that way. She just wanted to go home. Just wanted to rest, just wanted the stupid contractions to stop.

She had read that they were her uterus practicing for the real thing. She hoped it got a lot of practice in so the real thing went fast. She supposed she shouldn't begrudge the contractions if that's what they were doing.

The lady was not there when she opened the door, but she must have heard the latch click, because she called out as Skyler stepped out of the bathroom.

"Linda! Come on in the kitchen. I have some refreshments, and you know it's your favorite room in the house."

As soon as she said that, there was a crash in the back, and it sounded like an entire container of liquid had fallen to the floor.

Five

Skyler hurried toward the sound. She stepped into the kitchen, and the lady was on her hands and knees muttering to herself. "Oh no. What have I done? Oh no. What was I doing?"

She slowly got up. Then, she turned, took one look at Skyler, and screamed.

Skyler put up a hand. "It's okay. I'm Linda, remember?" She didn't know what else to say. The lady acted like she'd never seen her before in her life.

"Mom? Mom? Are you okay?"

A male voice came downstairs as Skyler stood frozen in the kitchen. She wanted to run.

Then there was the sound of steps on the stairs, quick and heavy like the man was jogging.

"There's an intruder in the house!" the woman in front of her screamed, her hand to her chest, her finger pointed directly at Skyler like Skyler had done something wrong. Skyler didn't know what to do, didn't know what to say. The woman... Had it been a trap?

She would just explain to the man that she had simply had to go to the bathroom.

"What's going on?" The man came into the room, saw his mother, and his eyes landed on Skyler. His brows drew down, and his eyes narrowed. "Who are you?"

"She broke into the house! I've never seen her before in my life! You've got to get her out of here!" The woman's words were shrill and panicked, and then she seemed to notice, as though for the first time, that Skyler was pregnant.

Her voice modulated but still didn't hold the affection it had before when she'd been calling Skyler Linda. "You're expecting. You know, you really should get your life together. You don't want your baby to see his mama going around from house to house stealing things!"

"How did that sweet tea get spilled on the floor?" the man asked, looking from Skyler to his mother and back to Skyler before he lifted a brow and looked at his mom.

For some reason, there was an expression on his face that gave Skyler the feeling that he wasn't expecting an answer.

"My goodness. There is sweet tea all over the floor!" The woman's face crumpled. "And my good glass pitcher is broken!"

"It's okay, Mom. We can get you another glass pitcher. Did you drop it?"

"I don't know," his mom said.

He looked at Skyler. Skyler put her hands up. "I promise. I was outside. I saw her in the garden. I asked if I could use the restroom because..." How was she supposed to say that her boyfriend... *fiancé* dropped her off and drove away from her? That was so embarrassing. It was like...like there was something wrong with her. Like she was so unlovable that the father of her baby couldn't stand to be with her and would drop her off in a no-name town and leave.

"I used the restroom. I promise I didn't break the pitcher or steal anything. She was calling me Linda."

The man's face registered understanding. "I see. All right, so you needed to use the restroom, and you're leaving?"

She nodded. Grateful that she wasn't getting accused of breaking the pitcher, because even though it probably wasn't extremely expensive, she didn't have a penny on her.

"All right. I'll take care of this. Can you see yourself out?" The man dismissed her abruptly and turned to his mother. "Here, Mom. Let me help you to a seat so you don't slip and fall. That would be the very last thing you need."

"Phil, I am perfectly capable of walking by myself."

Their voices faded as she walked out the door, closing it behind her. So much for a tour of the house. Not that she had time. Jeff was probably sitting outside in a vehicle, waiting for her right now.

It made her a little sad to leave the pretty house, although it was so confusing in there. The man's name must be Phil, since that's what the woman had called him, and she was his mom, and...maybe she had dementia or something. That would explain the odd way she had been treating Skyler. Not that Skyler knew too many people with dementia, but there were a couple that came into the diner with their caregivers.

Sometimes they called her by her right name. Sometimes they acted like they didn't know her.

She was familiar with that. She talked to the caregivers some. The casual conversation a waitress has with her patrons. Skyler's coworkers did it to get good tips, but Skyler did it because she was always interested in people and their stories. She always wondered what kind of story she'd make up for herself, if she were going to fill in the blank pages of her life and get herself a family, friends, a childhood.

She wanted to give herself the best. But she wasn't sure what that was. She put a hand on her stomach as it tightened with another contraction, hurrying to the gate, as clouds rolled darkly overhead and thunder rumbled ominously.

She tried to remain hopeful, anticipatory, as she opened the gate and stepped out, looking first up the street and then down.

Nothing. There was nothing.

The cramp, worse than all the other contractions put together, gripped her stomach so hard she thought she was going to fall over. She wasn't sure her legs would continue to hold her while it felt like some big hand had taken her entire insides and twisted it or balled it up like a piece of trash.

She put both hands around her stomach and doubled over, unable to stop the groan that came out of her mouth.

She thought, not for the first time, that if this was a Braxton Hicks contraction, she did not want to feel even one of the real thing.

And then, like her day couldn't get any worse, big, thick, heavy drops of rain started to fall. They hit her on the back, soaking through her thin shirt, plopping down into her hair, and making the pain that gripped her midsection that much worse.

Suddenly the day that had seemed so warm and welcoming just a few minutes ago, now seemed like it couldn't get any worse. She really wanted to get out of the rain.

Walking along the wrought iron fence, she came to the garage that she had seen earlier, and intended to stand under the overhang those types of structures typically had, except this one didn't have one.

So, putting her fingers in the crack between the doors, she pulled it open and stepped inside.

The pain from her midsection faded, and the rain stopped pounding on her.

It was dark inside, and something moved... Hopefully a cat. But she wasn't sure.

She didn't want to examine that thought. She would just...sit here until the rain ended. And then she would, she didn't know. The store lady was gone, and the house that she had just been in was so weird. The man did not look overly happy to see her, although he hadn't been unkind. But he had seemed a little harried, like he had been interrupted from something very important, and to top it off, he had the mess of the sweet tea to clean up.

Then, another pain gripped her, this one even worse than the last one if that were even possible, and she stumbled against the wall, leaning heavily on her side as waves of pain seemed to wash over her, in big, rolling vises, like she was stuck in a machine that was slowly grinding up her insides.

She closed her eyes and fought against it, and then she remembered vaguely something she'd read about breathing with the pain.

And then, she tried to remember if she had heard about anyone having to breathe through Braxton Hicks contractions.

They weren't supposed to hurt that bad.

She straightened, and it was then that she noticed that her maternity pants were a lot more wet than she would have expected from the amount of rain that she had been in.

She'd been bending over, so they shouldn't have gotten that way. The wind wasn't blowing strongly, not strong enough to blow it sideways and wet her jeans...

Had her water broke?

It was then that she knew that she was in labor, for sure.

Well, she was going to have to get out of the garage and get the people in the house to help her.

She turned around by what looked like a lawnmower, as her eyes had adjusted to the dim interior, and noticed a lawn chair folded up beside it.

There was a bag of something that could possibly be beach towels beside it, which made sense since they lived so close to Lake Michigan. Probably everybody had beach towels in their garage.

Regardless, it didn't matter, she was going to have to go in and get help.

Another contraction gripped her, hard, ripping, searing pain, and she bent over, thinking she would just wait until this one was over.

But then, there was a huge flash of light, so close it felt like it was right beside the garage, followed by an immediate clashing of thunder so loud she jumped despite the pain.

She couldn't step out in that! She would get electrocuted.

She would have to make do here. Although, lightning didn't strike the same place twice. Right? Did she read that somewhere?

If she was wrong, she could die walking from the garage to the house, and then, what if they didn't let her in? What if the lady screamed and pointed at her and said she was an intruder?

Maybe if the man had been more welcoming. Maybe if she hadn't seen the lightning, if either of those things hadn't happened, she might have walked across, but as it was, she felt it was too big of a risk.

So, between contractions, she unfolded the chair and rooted in the bag, seeing that it was, indeed, beach towels.

She worked between contractions as they came faster and faster, and maybe she had intended to sit in the chair and...she didn't know. Have the baby? Take a rest? Wait for the rain to stop?

She wasn't sure, she just knew that the contractions got harder and harder as the lightning started coming almost as fast, and the thunder made it sound like the storm was on top of her, making the contractions feel even worse until she was moaning through them, and then she felt the oddest urge to bear down, like she needed to have a bowel movement, and the contractions were so bad, worse than anything she'd ever felt before, and she found herself biting on her shirt to stifle her screams, and then she thought, *Who cares? Nobody cares!*

She screamed. As loud and long as she could, and it surprised her, since she didn't know she could make a sound like that, but it also took her mind off her pain and actually helped a little.

Except, it didn't get rid of the urge to bear down, and she wondered if that meant the baby was coming.

Six

Homer sat inside his study, his face in his hand.

He'd figured out the problem he'd been wrestling with before, finished the project, and sent it to his boss. His boss had been surprised, because he hadn't expected Homer to finish for at least another two weeks.

But the project had come together a lot faster than Homer had expected, and he wasn't one to draw things out until the last minute. His boss would most likely find another project for him or have him collaborate with someone else, but it would be a couple days. He would have known that Homer worked practically around the clock to finish what he had, and while the company wanted to make money, they didn't begrudge their employees for doing a good job.

His problem was not his work. Which was going better than it ever had.

His problem was his mother. She was getting worse. And worse and worse. She had invited a complete and absolute stranger into the house. For goodness only knew what. At least, according to the stranger, she'd been invited in. Of course, the girl had said that she had come in to use the bathroom, but he figured his mother was probably right. She had been set on stealing something, and his mom had just realized it, dropped the pitcher in shock, and then proceeded to completely forget that she had invited the person in.

Of course, the woman might have walked in without an invitation. His mother probably hadn't locked the door when she went out. And he needed to keep a better eye on her, because that wasn't the first time she wandered out. He needed to put locks on the doors that she couldn't open.

He hated to do that, to lock her in, but...he wasn't going to have a choice. Otherwise, he would never get anything done, because he would have to watch her all the time.

He pretty much already did. He got his best work done at night while she slept. *If* she slept, since she was awake at night a good bit, too.

Still, his mother had gone to bed; thankfully, she was early to bed, but she was also early to rise.

That suited his circadian rhythm just fine as well. He enjoyed watching the sunrise and the way it reflected on the lake.

Of course, the lake was west, or a little southwest, because of the inlet where the town was situated on, but the sunrise still showed on the lake in beautiful colors of pinks and oranges and blues as the water rippled and stirred.

Of course, he hadn't walked to the bluffs overlooking the lake to see the sunrise for quite some time. Not since his mother had gotten bad enough that he couldn't leave her alone.

Sometimes people came to help him watch her, but people typically weren't up before sunrise, thinking that a caretaker might want to have a little bit of time to watch God's glory at work in the morning.

He stood up from his desk, knowing that it had almost gotten to the point where he needed to hire someone. Someone to spend the day with his mother so he could get some work done.

Maybe just for a few hours. They could watch her during the morning, and he could handle the afternoon when she often took a nap, and then they'd have the evening together.

He'd have to look into that. It was probably expensive, but money wasn't exactly an issue. His mother had come from a wealthy family, and his dad had been a surgeon.

Of course, they didn't have his dad's income anymore, but he made pretty good money as a computer programmer.

Homer got up and walked to the window, looking over the garden toward the garage, down the street, freshly washed from the early spring thunderstorm that had blown through just a few minutes ago.

He loved the smell of the earth after the storm and lifted the window a little, letting the air in. His dad always had conniptions when they opened the windows, saying that they had central air for a reason. And in the Michigan winters, it made sense to keep the windows tightly closed. His dad would say he wasn't heating the outside after all. But his dad wasn't paying the bills anymore, hadn't been for quite some time. And Homer figured that it didn't matter. If he wanted to open the window and smell the freshly washed earth, he could.

He hadn't been standing there for more than fifteen seconds or so, breathing deeply, before he heard what sounded like a woman screaming.

That in itself was odd, but...it sounded like it was coming from his garage.

He thought of the girl that had been in his house earlier that day. Maybe she had some kind of pimp or handler that was torturing her because she wasn't able to steal anything valuable.

Homer shrugged that idea off. Not in Raspberry Ridge. There were like fifty people total in town. It wasn't a large place.

Of course, there were some people who lived on the farms outside of town, and ever since Blueberry Beach and Strawberry Sands had gotten bigger, there had been a few of the bad actors that that type of industry attracted.

But there it was again. It sounded like a woman was in agony.

There were guns in the house, but they were locked up, especially because of his mother, and he didn't take the time to unlock the gun cabinet to grab one. Instead, after he hurried downstairs, he took a poker from the fireplace in the formal living room.

There were several fireplaces in the house that worked, and they were nice and cozy on a cold winter night. But the poker would be nice and handy if there was someone in his garage.

Maybe it would end up coming from the beach below the bluffs, and he would be spared the duty of handling whatever it was. Maybe it was a cat.

Sometimes cats could sound like people.

Back when Michigan was a lot wilder and a lot less settled, there might have been panthers in the area. He'd heard they could sound like women too.

Not that he'd ever heard one.

He made it outside, walking along the garden path and pausing at the back door to the garage.

It looked like the garage doors that led out to the short driveway before it hit the street might have been opened. It still looked like there might have been a crack there. He couldn't tell for sure. Everything was dark. There was a light switch as soon as he walked in. So, he stood at the door, took a breath, then yanked the door open and flipped the lights immediately, poker raised, ready to do whatever was necessary to save the woman, if that's what it was, and run the bad actors out of his garage.

He supposed he could have called the police, but he left his cell phone upstairs, and Raspberry Ridge did not have their own force. Someone would have to come from Blueberry Beach, and it would take at least a half an hour.

Folks around Raspberry Ridge were used to handling their own problems.

Even folks like him, who typically sat behind a desk and worked at a computer all day long.

All of those thoughts were random in his head as he prepared to face whatever the light showed.

He had not been prepared for what he saw though.

He was pretty sure it was the girl from earlier, although she looked a lot different than she had. She still wore something on her top, but her bottoms had disappeared. She was half sitting, half reclining in a beach chair, and there was blood and other fluids staining her legs.

He was not a doctor, and he had never seen anything born, not even an animal give birth, but he was pretty sure he knew what was going on.

Ninety percent of him wanted to throw the poker down, spin

around, flip the lights off, and slam the door shut as he ran away. That ninety percent was what he had inherited from his father.

Thankfully, some of his mother's blood flowed in his veins, because she was the kind of person who didn't run away. And that was the kind of person that he determined he wanted to be. The kind of person who...didn't run.

God sure had an interesting way of testing a person's resolve, though. He had to hand it to Him.

He hadn't seen too many things that had given him a greater desire to get out of Dixie.

The woman's eyes were huge, her mouth open, as though she had been ready to let out another scream. Then her face scrunched up, and as he watched, her whole body crumbled, and she fell in on herself, her head curled around her stomach, her hands gripping the arms of the chair.

It was almost like watching a car accident. He just wanted to stand there and stare, but he couldn't. He couldn't just stand there.

Hurrying around the tubs that were neatly labeled in his mother's handwriting, which had gotten squiggly with her disease, he hurried to the lawn chair and hesitated before he knelt on one knee. The woman groaned loud and low, her entire body looking like a spring about ready to pop out of a jack-in-the-box.

"Tell me how I can help," he said.

She didn't say anything. Just groaned.

"I left my phone inside. I can call 911." He didn't want to leave her for that long though. She looked like the baby was coming. He thought he saw it. Dark hair. It...was a little uncomfortable, now that he was closer to her, but he supposed that birth was one of those times when the modesty dictates of society weren't necessarily in effect.

It looked like she was relaxing, like maybe the pain she was in was going away.

"You want to go inside?"

"I don't think there's time. I think... I think I felt the baby's head."

He nodded. Although she wasn't looking at him. He thought he *saw* the baby's head. So, they were on the same page about that, anyway.

Well. He kind of wished his boss had returned his email immediately with the hardest problem that anyone in the company had ever faced. He thought it would be easy compared to what he was doing right now. Which was trying to figure out how to help a woman have a baby, without his phone to Google anything, and trying to figure out if he could be held liable if he left her and something happened.

"You have a phone?" Maybe he could call on her phone.

"No. No phone. No money. Nothing. Sorry. I didn't mean to do this." The last words were said on a squeak as another contraction seemed to tear through her. He could almost see it wrapping around her as she raised herself against it and curled around her stomach again, her hands on the armrests.

Maybe he should offer her his hand, but from the whiteness of her knuckles, he almost thought that she might squeeze it right off.

"I have no idea what to do. None. I... I can program your phone or your computer if you want me to, but this...this is not my wheelhouse. It's not my boat, not my ocean, not my universe."

The woman was not listening to him, and typically he did not have a problem rambling on, but his hands were sweating, and there was some kind of caterpillar-like thing crawling up the back of his neck, possibly what used to be his backbone. He felt uncomfortable, making him want to dance like his clothes were on fire or something.

Dance right out of the garage.

Finally, he thought to himself, *What would Mom do?*

Over the course of his life, when he'd run into a situation where he wasn't sure what the right thing was, he always tried to think about what his mom would do. She was closer to Jesus than anyone else he knew, and if someone was going to choose the right thing, it would be her.

Immediately he knew exactly what she would do.

He rolled up his sleeves and said to the woman as her grip slowly loosened on the arms of the chair, "I think you're going to need to lie back a little more."

She didn't say anything, and he adjusted the arms of the chair so she leaned back slightly more. Maybe it was good for her to curl over her stomach. Maybe that was helpful to push, although she didn't seem like she was pushing, she just seemed like she was fighting the contractions.

But if that was the top of the baby's head that he saw, it was definitely time to push.

He knew that much. But he was really dredging down into the recesses of his brain, back when he had stayed home from school, which hadn't been very often, he'd rarely been sick, and while he hadn't loved school, he hadn't hated it either, and he'd just gone, since that's what he was supposed to do. But on the few times that he hadn't, he remembered lying on the couch while his mom watched some kind of baby show. Where the camera followed a couple through pregnancy, from learning that they were going to have a baby, to getting the baby's room ready, to the labor at the very end.

He tried to think about what he learned on the show, although the show never showed anything like he had just seen. Like what he was looking at now.

It all had been nicely fuzzed out, to spare his childish eyes and sensitive, delicate, childish sensibilities.

Unfortunately.

Since now, he really could have used the knowledge.

"I'm going to try to catch the baby. I... I think you need to push with the next contraction."

"I have towels," the woman said, sounding a little breathless and completely exhausted. Which well she should. He didn't know much, but having a baby had to be exhausting.

But this must have happened pretty suddenly. He didn't think she was in labor when she was in the house earlier, but come to think of it, he hadn't spent much time looking at her and had been a little rude.

A lot rude. His mother would never have acted the way he did.

He reached over and grabbed a towel from the stack she pointed out, recognizing it as one of his favorite beach towels.

Interesting. She'd made herself at home. Which, there was a whole pile of questions in his mind, but they didn't really have to do with what he was trying to do right now, which was deliver the baby and hopefully not let it die.

If anything happened, he tried to think about how long it would take him to sprint into the house, run up the stairs, and grab his cell phone. He wished he would have done that immediately when he saw the woman, but...sometimes people just didn't make the right decisions. Sometimes once those decisions were made, right or wrong, he had to go with them. And now was not the time to decide he needed his phone. He definitely couldn't leave her now, because another contraction was stealing over her, her grip tightened, her body curled, and this time, she was pushing.

Yeah. It was...very painful looking.

And slow.

That contraction eased, and she relaxed.

"Is it here?"

She sounded like she was still in pain, still straining, and he said, "No. It's not."

"Another," she said immediately and curled again.

It was a while until the baby was there. At least fifteen minutes, maybe more. But he didn't have his phone and couldn't time it. He just knew one contraction seemed to roll into another one, and the woman was tired, and he was tempted to...help. He lost most of his modesty, but the idea of touching her... He knew he was going to have to eventually, but he waited until the head was mostly out, and then he supported it with one hand.

He wasn't quite sure how the shoulders were supposed to come, and whether he needed to move the baby at all so that the shoulders would slide out, but apparently whatever he did was okay, and the rest of the baby came without too much trouble.

He forgot about the umbilical cord. The baby was still attached. He had nothing to cut it with, nothing except a towel to hold it with.

Wait, he had to make sure it was breathing.

Before he cut the cord, was the baby...

"Wipe his nose. Quick."

He did kind of remember on the show there being some kind of blue ball thing that they stuffed up the baby's nose to pull the gunk out, but he didn't have anything like that, so he used an end of the towel to swipe at the gunk in his nose and from around his mouth. Apparently, that was all he needed to do, since the baby shivered and shook and maybe sneezed, although he couldn't quite tell, and then he let out a scream like Homer had just stolen his Lamborghini. Or his baby rattle.

He was breathing. That was good. Screaming meant alive.

He remembered his mother saying that in the church nursery.

Funny the times his mother's voice came into his head.

"Can you hold him? I don't have any way of tying the cord or cutting it. And...I can grab my phone too. Can I have three minutes?"

He could do it all in three minutes. He wasn't sure whether regular scissors would cut that, and he wasn't sure what he could tie it off with. He thought he had wire ties. Could he sanitize the wire ties somehow?

He hadn't washed his hands, hadn't realized that he was going to deliver a baby, or maybe he would have been a little bit more prepared.

That was hindsight again.

"Yeah. I think so."

Her voice was weak and soft, and her eyes hadn't left her baby. He carefully set it on her stomach, and as her hands came around it, making sure it wouldn't fall off, his gaze went to her face.

There was no question she loved the little one on top of her. Of course. It came from her body. But her gaze was so tender, so filled with awe, so amazed, it made his heart swell to watch. And he felt a little bit like he was eavesdropping on a silent conversation that should have been private.

Or maybe, something between the woman and her husband and the baby. The baby's father, since he didn't see a ring on any of the woman's fingers.

"I'll be right back," he said, realizing that his hands were covered in goop, and he didn't want to rub them down his leg, but he also didn't know if he could even get the garage doorknob to turn with that kind of slime on him. He hadn't realized that birth included slime.

He hadn't realized he was going to learn that today either.

Life had a way of surprising people sometimes.

Skyler stared at the baby on her stomach.

In her heart, she knew that she shouldn't be looking at the tiny little thing, who was crying at the top of his lungs, and think he was the most beautiful thing that she'd ever seen.

But he was. Perfect little hands, scrunched-up eyes, a face that was maybe a little misshapen but still beautiful. With sweet, pudgy cheeks and a cute, chubby chin.

The whole body was chubby. She looked at the belly, where the umbilical cord was still attached.

Nothing she had read had told her how to handle the umbilical cord. Probably because that was the hospital's job.

But...that man, the one who had been brusque with her before, had delivered her baby.

She could hardly believe it, and now that her baby was out, she was a little embarrassed about the whole situation.

Moving a little bit, she grabbed a towel from the stack and threw it over her legs.

Maybe there were some other things that needed to be done, but she had no idea. She just wanted someone else to make the decisions. She'd had quite a day. *Quite* a day.

"Is someone dying in here?" a voice said as the garage doors opened. They let in a little light from a streetlight that was on the other side of the street somewhere.

"Just me. I had a baby."

She could hardly believe it. But it was true. She had a baby.

"I'm sorry. I thought you just said you had a baby." The woman paused as though processing that information, testing it as to its accuracy. "Hang on, let me move back through these things."

"It's true. That's what I said. I... I guess I might have been a little bit loud, but I wasn't expecting it to hurt so bad."

"I'm sorry. You just had a baby?" The woman didn't sound like she believed her, and then she came out from between two stacks of tubs.

"Oh my goodness. I think you did have a baby. Oh, and she's shivering." Her voice changed on that last line, and she went into mom or doctor mode or whatever, because she came over, grabbed a towel from the stack, and said, "We need to wrap this little girl up."

"It's a boy," Skyler corrected her.

"I'm sorry, sweetheart, this is a girl all day long." She cleared her throat. "I know there are some people who are confused, but biology is biology, and we've got to believe the science, right?" She held the baby up, and Skyler looked.

It was a girl.

"But...my mother's intuition." Had been wrong.

"Well, I'm not sure what you're saying, but this little girl is still attached. What's going on here?"

"I don't know. But I think I need to push again." She didn't mean to say that, but the urge to push came over her, and a contraction, and... that was weird.

"Oh, you're probably going to deliver the placenta. All right. Well, this was not what I was expecting to do this evening, and it's not exactly in my line of work, which is design, in case you were wondering, but... did you do this by yourself?" the lady said as she moved things around and handed Skyler her baby back, now wrapped up tightly in a towel, her body completely covered, although the umbilical cord came out the side.

"The guy who delivered her is coming back with scissors and a clip," she said, realizing she'd answered the question and also trying to let her know that she didn't have to do anything drastic, because they were going to be able to cut the cord. They just needed a little bit of time.

She wasn't sure whether it was bad for the baby to stay connected or not.

She wanted her baby to have the very best. Her baby...girl. That was a shock. She hadn't even thought about girl names. She'd been so sure it was going to be a boy. She'd bought brown blankets at the secondhand store, for goodness' sake.

"All right. If you get the urge to push, just go ahead and do it. I think that will deliver the afterbirth."

The lady didn't bat an eye as she moved around Skyler, like she'd done it all before, although maybe she'd been in Skyler's position when it happened. Since she said she was into design and not nursing, or midwifery, or an obstetrician.

"I have wire ties and scissors." The man was back, and he spoke as he walked in, then he stopped abruptly. "Miss Vera. This is probably not what you expected to see in my garage."

"Hello, Homer. I think you have some explaining to do. Are you the one who's responsible for this baby?"

"I promise you, Miss Vera. I did the best I could. You know I'm a computer programmer. Delivering babies isn't—"

"I wasn't talking about that. Are you the one who got this girl pregnant?"

"No!" Homer had reached her side, but he backed up a step, holding his hands up, with all the paraphernalia dangling from them. "I promise. I never saw her before in my life. Except—"

"Except?" Vera prodded.

"I was in his house earlier today. His mom let me go to the bathroom. She called me Linda."

It still seemed kind of odd.

"She has Alzheimer's," Homer said softly. "She probably mistook you for one of her friends that she used to have Bible study with. She... had an affair with Mom's husband, and I think Mom was getting you guys confused because of you being pregnant."

"Oh." She had figured some of that, the Alzheimer's, but to have him confirm it made everything make sense.

"All right. Let's put these wire ties on. I'm pretty sure that's not what they typically use to tie the cord off, but it'll work," Vera said, all business again.

She and Homer worked quietly together, every once in a while murmuring a command or question, as they tied the cord off, and then Vera pointed at the scissors.

"Did you sanitize those?"

"I brought some Clorox wipes out," he said, picking up the container where it had fallen on the floor. "I didn't know what else to do."

"That'll have to do for now. I'm pretty sure we need to cut it. And then, I do think that she's going to need to go to the emergency room, just to have everything checked out. Make sure the baby's okay. Have her weighed and everything."

"I don't want to go." Skyler spoke softly, even though they weren't really talking to her.

"You might not want to go, sweetheart, but you have a baby to think about now. And you need to have her checked out. They're supposed to give them a vitamin K shot, and I think they usually put something in their eyes too, but I forget what it is." Her brows furrowed, and she paused for a moment as though thinking, then she shook her head and continued to work with Homer.

"We probably ought to get a pan and put the afterbirth in it. The doctor might want to examine it to make sure it's all there. I know they do that with horses, but... I can't remember what they do with babies. Or maybe I wasn't paying attention, because I was totally in love with mine." Her voice trailed off, as though it were a sad memory.

"I'm sorry, ma'am."

"It's okay. They're good memories. And it's okay to relive them."

But just the way she said it made it sound like there were sad memories too, and the two were mixed together.

Sometimes that happened in life. What could be the worst day of her life, with her boyfriend, *fiancé*—maybe *ex*-fiancé?—leaving her alone in a town and never coming back, and then the birth of her baby, which was the best thing that ever happened to her.

"Is there a red pickup outside?" she asked, thinking for the first time that maybe since she stepped in the garage, Jeff hadn't been able to find her.

"I haven't seen any red pickups. Did you drive here? I... I suppose it's only natural for us to wonder what in the world is going on. I mean, you just had a baby in somebody's garage. And neither one of us have ever seen you before."

"I know. It's a long story, and I'm kind of embarrassed."

"Well, we all do embarrassing things. That's part of being a human. You're not going to escape life without it, unless you die young..." Again, her voice trailed off.

"Do I have to go to the hospital? I don't have money to pay for it." There. She was just being honest.

"Let's get you to the hospital, and we'll worry about the money later. It's important that the baby gets checked out at least, and we want to make sure that you didn't tear or anything. I believe if they're going to fix that, they need to do it quickly."

Out of everything that she'd been through that day, it was funny that Vera's words would make her blush now, but she could feel her cheeks heating as she held her baby close.

Her cries had stopped shortly after Homer had put her in her arms, and she just wanted to sit and bond with her baby. Make the rest of the world go away. Although she knew that wasn't reasonable, a person couldn't just sit in someone's garage, in a chair that wasn't theirs, with basically no clothes on, cuddling their baby and not facing the fact that they were an adult and they had to do life.

"You want to go ahead and bring your car around? You can take her to the hospital." Vera spoke to Homer.

It hadn't occurred to Skyler to think that there was no car in the garage. Just lawnmowers and tubs full of things, and other big, honking things with sheets thrown over them.

"Me?" Homer said, which made Skyler's eyes open wide. Vera wanted Homer to take her to the hospital?

"Well, who else is going to take her?"

"You?" Homer said, sounding more hopeful than determined.

"Doesn't someone need to stay with your mother?" Vera asked.

"Yeah. I probably should stay with my mother. Good point."

"The doctors might want to know what exactly went on. I'm going to assume that Skyler was in a lot of pain and can't be as lucid as you if the doctors have questions. I, on the other hand, was not here and could not answer those questions. Plus, this is your garage, therefore, anyone who has a baby in it is your responsibility."

If Skyler had felt a little better, she might have tried a little harder to figure out if it was humor in Vera's voice, or if she really didn't want to take her to the hospital. She thought it was humor though. Like she was laughing a little at the fact that Homer was going to have to take her. But Skyler was embarrassed. She didn't want to put the man out. She'd already uprooted his day. After all, no one got up in the morning thinking that they were going to deliver a baby in their garage that day. Literally no one.

"All right. I'll bring it around."

"Thank you. We'll try to get her ready to move. After I had my baby, they had me up and moving around within an hour. I would think that you would be able to get up and walk. Do you think you can?" Vera said, and her voice was gentle, as was her hand that landed on Skyler's shoulder.

"I think so." She didn't see any reason why she couldn't. She was definitely a little sore, feeling a little weak and tired, and there was also a stranger feeling that she felt as well. Maybe because of seeing her daughter for the first time. Daughter. She couldn't believe she had been wrong.

"How about I hold the baby while you try to get up? I'll try to keep my arm around you, but I don't want anything to happen to the baby. That's why I'll hold her. If you think you're going to fall or pass out, just let your knees buckle and fall back down on the chair, okay?"

"Yeah." That made sense. She could make sure she fell in the chair. She didn't want to hurt the baby. She handed her to Vera and then tried to grab hold of the towels.

"I'll make sure you get a towel wrapped around your waist. In the meantime, don't worry about modesty as much as just getting up and getting on your feet. Okay?"

She hadn't been worried about modesty, not when she was in the middle of childbirth, but now that it was over, all her modesty had come rushing back, along with a lot of embarrassment. Homer had...yeah. He had seen her with her clothes off. That was...embarrassing.

But her baby was fine, and she should be happy about that. And probably neither Homer nor she would ever talk about it, and maybe eventually they'd both forget.

No. Absolutely not. She didn't figure either one of them would ever forget anything.

Regardless, she tried to push that away. She wasn't going to think about it. She had other things to focus on, and currently that was standing up.

She hadn't realized how weak she was, and she was so thirsty.

She didn't want to complain though, so she didn't ask for a drink, and she took Vera's proffered arm, using it to steady herself as she stood slowly to her feet.

"Ah. The resiliency of youth," Vera said breezily as Skyler stood trembling beside her

"I'm honestly not sure how long I can stand here. I feel a lot weaker than I expected to."

"You're so skinny, you're probably used to leaning a little on the baby to keep you up. Now that's gone, you have to hold yourself up again."

Vera didn't say how she knew that, but she did grab a towel.

"Do you think you have enough strength to hold your baby while I wrap this around your waist? I'll try to tuck it in, so you have a little bit of modesty while you're walking."

"Thanks. My pants are around somewhere, but they were wet."

"Yeah. That's understandable. There's probably blood on them too. I... I might be able to run to my house and grab some clothes for you, or maybe Homer will have a pair of sweatpants or something you can put on at the hospital. I don't think you have to worry about it right now. They're just going to make you take them off there anyway, and you're going to need something to protect them."

She said that last line a little delicately, and Skyler wasn't quite sure what she meant, but she could hazard a guess.

"I never thought about that."

"Neither did I. That was kind of a surprise. But you should probably expect it for two to four weeks."

Two to four weeks? She didn't even have a pair of underwear, let alone money to buy any or money to buy "protection" as Vera so delicately put it.

There was definitely a lot more to this than what she was expecting.

Not that she expected to have her baby in a garage. And without her...ex. She probably ought to start thinking about Jeff as an ex. Even if he hadn't dumped her, she wasn't sure that it was wise for her to continue to be with someone who could leave her along the side of the road with absolutely nothing. It wasn't like her purse was hidden underneath the seat where he wouldn't see it. It was sitting on top of her seat, where he would know that she didn't have any money, any cards, any phone, any anything.

And yet he'd left. Completely and totally left. It must be after midnight. She had no idea, other than it had been dark for a while.

And he hadn't come back. From the looks of things, he wasn't planning on coming back. She...couldn't believe it.

The car motor interrupted her thoughts as Vera took her baby back away from her.

"I'll carry her to the car. You really should have a car seat, but I don't."

"I actually do. But it's in Chicago."

"Is that where you're from?"

"Yeah. I lived there all my life. This is the second time I've been out of town. And the furthest I've been away from home."

"Is there someone I should call? Do you have a phone?"

"I don't have a phone, and no, there's no one to call."

Her voice cracked a little on that last word. She hadn't thought about how alone she was in the world. But with Jeff leaving her stranded, she couldn't count on him. She had her coworkers at the diner, but Kylie had been her best friend.

She swallowed. She was going to do better. She was going to create a life for this baby, somehow. She wasn't sure exactly how, but somehow, someway, somewhere.

It seemed like a good time to pray, but she never wanted to be one of those people who didn't talk to God until she needed Him, wasn't nice to someone until she needed them. Not that she didn't pray. She prayed a lot, but this was different. This was...desperate.

She supposed if there was ever a time for her to pray, it would be now.

Lord, I know I haven't spent a lot of time going to church or anything like that. Maybe You only listen to people who go to church, but in case You're going to listen to me, I... I want to make a better life for my baby. I want her to have a better life than I had. I want her to have a family. I wanted her to have a dad. A dad who loves her. I wasn't planning on having a baby.

There she stopped. God was probably up there with His arms crossed, going, "What did you think was going to happen when you had sex with your boyfriend?" Even if she was on the pill. But premarital sex was still wrong. Whether she was on the pill or not. Getting caught didn't make it all of a sudden a sin. Being pregnant wasn't the sin. It was the activity that came before.

I'm sorry, Lord. You're right. I shouldn't have been doing that. Now, I guess I'm paying the price, and I'm fine with paying the price, but please don't make my baby pay the price. Please?

She had a feeling that the Lord wasn't listening. But just in case she was wrong, she added an *amen* while Homer came into the garage.

"I don't think she's strong enough to walk that far. At least I think you should have your arm around her, ready to catch her if she needs it."

"All right," Homer said, and he came over and put his arm around her without hesitating. She liked the way he had rolled up his sleeves and delivered her baby without hesitating. She liked a man who wasn't going to see a problem and run from it. Too bad Jeff wasn't that kind of man.

"All right. We have no car seat, so if you get stopped by the police, you're going to have to explain what's going on. It's not safe to drive without one, but I don't think we have a choice in this situation. I'm sure the police will understand, and...drive carefully."

Vera could have said, "don't be in an accident," but that was probably the reason they were called accidents. Because nobody meant to be in them.

But she didn't say that, didn't drag anything out, she just stood, watching as Homer helped Skyler in the car. He was stronger than he looked, not that he didn't look strong, he just didn't have bulging muscles or tons of tattoos or piercings, like the guys that she was used to seeing. Seemed like the more tattoos or piercings a person had, the tougher they thought they were. Maybe that was cliché. Her life was a whole pile of clichés though, so what was one more?

Still, he was harder than Jeff, and also his touch was more gentle. More gentle than Jeff on his most gentle day.

"Careful of your head. I can't put my hand over it so you don't hit it."

She'd seen police do that to people in handcuffs getting in the cop car, and maybe that's where Homer got it. She wasn't sure, but she appreciated the gentleness, the consideration. That, more than anything else, caused her eyes to prick.

No. Not that again. She wasn't pregnant anymore; she wasn't supposed to cry at the drop of a hat now. Or at the touch of someone who gave her the unfamiliar touch of gentleness and consideration.

He helped her in the car, and then Vera leaned in, handing her baby to her.

"You'll let me know how you are, somehow, right? I want to know, and just in case they don't let you come home, I just want to know."

"Of course," she said. "Thank you." She lifted her eyes and met Vera's in the dash light of the car.

Then, Vera stepped back and closed the door.

Skyler would not cry. She would not.

Eight

Homer kept his hands on the wheel, trying to make sure that he was extra vigilant in his driving. He didn't want anything to happen to the baby. He had turned the passenger seat airbag off at Vera's suggestion, and now all he had to do was make sure that he drove the same way he'd driven all his life. He'd never been in an accident up until that point, but he never had this kind of pressure on him either.

Responsible for a new, fragile, delicate, helpless little life that would be crushed out with even a little fender bender most likely.

"I'm going to the hospital in Blueberry Beach. It's the closest."

"That's fine." Her voice was soft and small. He wanted to reassure her everything would be okay, but he didn't know her circumstances and didn't want to promise things he wasn't sure were true.

"Do you have a preference?"

"No. I am...from Chicago. I've heard of Blueberry Beach, but I don't know anything about the hospital."

"I think Vera was right. You really should have the baby checked out at least."

"I agree. I just... I don't have any money."

"Don't worry about that. I'm not a billionaire or anything, but I think I can pay for a doctor's visit. So, you're covered, okay? So no more worrying about that." God didn't very often drop opportunities to help someone right in his lap, so if that happened, he'd better step up and take care of it.

"Okay." Her voice was soft. He wanted to do more to reassure her. To let her know that she didn't have anything to worry about. Except, it wasn't his responsibility. Of course, Miss Vera said that if a person had a baby in your garage, then you were responsible for them, but that was ridiculous.

He helped as much as he could, and now he was going to take her to the doctor's and...drop her off? Was he going to leave them?

He couldn't leave her there with no money.

"Do you have some family I should call? I've got my cell phone, and you can make a call."

"No." The word was quiet but very final.

"You don't have any family at all?"

"No."

"You were hatched?" He didn't mean to be sarcastic, but come on, she had a mom.

"I was a foster kid. I aged out, and they kicked me out. End of story."

"Whoa." So, maybe she did hatch.

That was not the answer he was expecting, but it made sense.

"Friends? Do you have any friends you could call?"

"No."

All right. So, he supposed he should just come out and ask, since it seemed to be his last resort.

"What about the father of the baby?"

"He dropped me off here today. I had to go to the bathroom. He stopped, and I went into the store that was open down the street. I went to the bathroom and walked down the aisle looking at the merchandise. I wanted to buy something in thanks for the lady letting me use her private restroom. But I couldn't afford it. So, ten minutes, tops, I was in that store. When I came out, he was gone. He hasn't come back."

"Oh."

Well, that answered that question.

"Maybe he was in a car accident?"

"Yeah. I guess I would have seen his smashed truck along the street in Raspberry Ridge if he had been in an accident and not driving away from me."

"Good point."

It did look bad, but sometimes things looked worse than what they were, or sometimes, there was a different explanation than the one that seemed the most obvious. He knew that much from computer programming.

But he couldn't think of another explanation.

"Did you have your purse? ID?"

"My purse was sitting on top of the seat. I remember looking at it and thinking I should take it, but I didn't really have any money to buy anything, and so I let it sit there. He...had to have seen it. It's not like he could forget about his pregnant fiancée."

"So...you're planning on getting married?"

"He asked me." She looked down at her fingers. "He bought a small ring, but I quit wearing it when my fingers swelled with the pregnancy."

She didn't seem like she was a spitfire earlier. But maybe her true personality was coming out, or maybe she was just angry, as he would be, if someone who was supposed to love him had left him by the side of the road, knowing he was a foster kid with no family and knowing he had no friends.

"Do you really have no friends?"

"My best friend died a month ago."

That pretty much answered all of his questions.

He imagined as a foster kid she might have moved from house to house, and perhaps she had learned not to make a lot of friends. He really wasn't sure.

He hadn't had too much contact with foster children.

He swallowed, looking back at the road. He wasn't going to be able to leave her at the hospital. He was going to have to take her home with him, but then what? What was he going to do with her then? And the baby? He already had his mom to take care of. He couldn't take care of a woman and her baby. How long was it going to take for her to get back on her feet?

A month? Two?

He had no idea how long it took a woman to recover from childbirth. But from what he had seen, he'd guess it would take her at least two months. Maybe three. It had looked painful and not like something he would ever want to do.

Silence filled the car as he drove through the night. He could see lightning flashing in the distance, lighting up clouds, and figured there were probably more thunderstorms rolling through. Lightning had struck in the yard and his garden just a few hours ago when the last one had come through. It was a good thing that she had found shelter in the garage, or she might have been hit.

As it was, he had been surprised the lights stayed on after a hit that close.

"I do have my high school diploma," Skyler said, as though she were defensive about it.

He hadn't asked, hadn't expected her to say anything. He noticed that she fingered the edge of the towel that she had wrapped around her waist.

"Well, that's good." His words lacked confidence since he wasn't quite sure why she'd even brought it up.

"I suppose you're a rocket scientist or something," she said, with not a little irritation in her voice. He wasn't sure what he had done to make her mad.

"Actually, not quite. I design computer programs for rocket scientists."

That was the truth. It was what he did. Sometimes he did it on his own, sometimes he worked in a group, sometimes he took what someone else had started, added some things to it, and sent it on down the line. Computer programming was not something that was fixed, but it could be fluid. Depending on the needs and what their clients wanted. Of course, there weren't a whole lot of rocket scientists, so the clientele was rather exclusive. His pay was rather exclusive as well, and paying for a short stay in the hospital would not set him back.

He tapped his finger on the steering wheel. He really hadn't given that much to the community. He'd been very content to stay in his study, work on his computer programming, and take care of his mother.

This would be his good deed for the day. The week. Maybe even the month. Depending on how expensive it was, it could even be for the year.

He was feeling rather good about himself.

But then he thought about how she didn't have a family, didn't have anyone.

Actually, maybe her loser dad had left before she was born and didn't wait until she was eighteen to get a girlfriend and leave his family. And that mirrored his own life too closely and turned his good feeling into a feeling like he wasn't doing enough.

What more do You want me to do, Lord?

Nine

Homer pulled into the hospital lot, using a handicap place to park. He didn't have a decal on his car, but Skyler figured that she was probably about as handicapped as a person could be at this point in her life.

Still, she had to protest. "I can walk from a regular spot."

"I was going to park right in front of the door, but I want to be able to go in with you, and if I do that, they'll let me take you in, but then I'll have to go move the car."

"Oh."

She didn't know why he would be so insistent that he had to go in with her. She was not exactly used to being alone, but she'd been alone for so long that she just assumed that she would be doing things by herself. She hadn't expected Homer to take her to the hospital and to want to continue on into the hospital with her.

Actually, she thought he would be pitching a fit about the possibility that she might be getting his seat so messy.

She was glad Vera had chosen such a big beach towel, one that went the whole way down to her ankles. She felt like she needed it. But she didn't know how much protection it was for the seat.

Jeff had been fanatically careful about his truck. Skyler had to wipe her shoes off before she was allowed to get in. And she definitely was not allowed to spill anything on it. He didn't like it when she put her feet on the dash, even if she took her shoes off first.

She often felt like his truck meant more to him than she did.

Maybe it did. After all, when he left town, he took his truck with him.

"Hello? Can I help you?" The clerk sitting behind the counter at the emergency room entrance looked up and spoke as they walked in together.

Skyler wasn't quite sure what to say, and she held her baby close, grateful that she had been quiet. She didn't really know how to take care of a baby, and she wasn't sure she wanted to learn in the car with Homer on the way to the hospital, especially when she didn't have a car seat. She didn't know if crying would make him angry, but she suspected it would. Jeff had not been happy about the idea of the baby crying.

While she hesitated, Homer stepped forward. "Skyler has just had a baby. We delivered her in my garage, but as soon as the storm passed and we were able to get in the car, we thought we needed to come to the hospital to have everyone checked out. Even though the baby and she both seem fine."

"Oh!" The lady's mouth held that shocked look for several long moments. Then she snapped into action. "All right." She shuffled a few papers around and then said, "We'll get your wife back to be seen immediately, along with the baby. The doctor will want to see them as soon as possible. If you can stay out here and fill out some paperwork for me, I'll take you right back to her. I promise you won't be separated for long." She stood as she was saying that, coming around the side of the counter, grabbing a wheelchair that was sitting beside it, and bringing it over to Skyler.

Skyler's mouth was going up and down, but she couldn't seem to get the words out. And Homer had started this conversation. Wasn't it his responsibility to correct this woman?

"Sweetheart. Please sit down. We need to get you to the back as soon as possible. You're lucky tonight. It's been quiet, and the doctor will be able to see you right away. I know you're going to want to get that little one checked out to make sure she's all fine and dandy. Congratulations, by the way," the woman chattered on as she pushed Skyler away.

Skyler looked back at Homer, who looked a little lost.

She resisted the urge to giggle, although it was not the slightest bit funny. But while Homer was a grown man and didn't seem to be shy, at times he seemed like maybe he spent a little bit too much time behind his computer and didn't quite know how to operate in the real world.

Skyler felt like she was ages older than him in that regard, although he must be a million times smarter than she was.

She had been kidding about the rocket science. But he had been dead serious. It was all she could do not to facepalm.

"Did you notice anything unusual about the birth?" the lady said as she pushed the wheelchair forward, the sliding glass doors closing with a thud behind them.

She must have noticed that Skyler was still turned around, looking at Homer, who was watching her disappear.

"Oh, honey, I promise, Daddy will be back with you soon. Is this your first baby? Then probably you didn't notice anything unusual. Everything was unusual." She chuckled softly, like childbirth wasn't one massive pain after another, with blood and bodily fluids flying everywhere, and like there was actually something funny about it.

Skyler couldn't think of a single funny thing. It was embarrassing, painful, uncomfortable, and pretty much every other bad adjective she could think of. The only thing good about it was... She looked down at her baby. Her beautiful, perfect, sleeping baby. She had one little fist tucked up underneath her cheek. Vera had wrapped the towel tightly around her so she was all curled up in a tight little ball.

Maybe Skyler should loosen the towel a bit. She was awfully tight. But she didn't really want to make the baby cry.

"What did you name her?" the receptionist asked as she pushed Skyler into the first available room.

Skyler didn't have an answer. She had been expecting a boy. Thankfully, the receptionist didn't wait.

"All right. I'll tell the doctor that this was your first baby, and you didn't notice anything unusual about the birth and everything seemed normal. He'll be in to see you, but first a nurse will probably come in and take her blood pressure and yours and all of that. All right, honey?"

The receptionist waited just a second as though Skyler was going to be able to get her scattered wits about her and say something before she charged back out of the room.

Maybe she was in a big rush to get Homer back there. The idea made Skyler want to rush to get into the little gown that the receptionist laid on the hard white hospital bed before she walked back out. She hadn't been joking that things were quiet. Which was nice.

She eyed the bed. Could she lay the baby down on it?

She wasn't sure. She kind of just wished she could sit and be undisturbed for days, maybe weeks. If someone would just bring her food.

That wasn't the way the world worked, though, and she knew that.

Feeling the aches and pains of the day and realizing she was more exhausted than what she realized, she slowly pushed her way out of the wheelchair and hesitated for just a moment before she laid her baby on the bed and changed into the gown.

She definitely needed the protection that Vera had talked about and figured she probably ought to bring that up with the doctor.

She didn't have anything. No money, no purse, no protection. And she didn't even have a way to get to the store to get any. That was one thing she hadn't seen in the store she'd walked through earlier in Raspberry Ridge. It had all been touristy things, beach things, souvenirs, that type of thing.

She took a look at her baby, and the urge to cry stole over her again. Harder than before, maybe because she was so tired.

She picked her baby back up and thought about feeding her.

It was supposed to be a natural thing, but she had no idea of where to even get started with it.

Plus, her baby hadn't opened her eyes almost since Vera had wrapped her in the towel. She obviously wasn't hungry. Maybe there was something wrong with her. A baby should be hungry, shouldn't it?

"Hey. I got here as soon as I could."

"I'm sorry about what she assumed," Skyler said immediately when

Homer popped his head in the door. She was glad she had changed quickly.

She settled herself on the edge of the hospital bed, squishing back from side to side, unwilling to put her baby back down.

"I had some paperwork to fill out, and I didn't know your last name, and I didn't know what you named the baby."

"I don't have a name for her. I was expecting a boy. What do you think?"

Homer blinked for a minute, as though surprised that she would be asking him, and rightfully so. Since they'd just met that day, and in some rather awkward circumstances, but unlike Jeff, once he got over the surprise of being asked, he tilted his head and looked at her face.

"No offense, but she looks a little bit like a monkey."

"I thought that too. But a beautiful monkey," Skyler said, laughing a little. She appreciated the fact that Homer was honest but in a sweet way; he didn't spit out the words that her baby was ugly and looked like a monkey. The way Jeff might have.

"I was thinking about April, since it's April."

"Tomorrow's the first day of May." Homer tilted his head. "But she was still born in April."

"Yeah. I guess May would be an okay name too."

"What about your mother's—" Homer broke off quickly. "Sorry. Forgot."

"No. That's okay. I'm not...like normal people. I don't have any relatives to name her after. Just me. And I don't want to give her my name. But I want her to have a pretty name. One that she will love all her life." She could name her after her gram, but they hadn't been close.

"I'll just admit that I'm not very good at coming up with stuff like this, but I like April okay. She wouldn't forget what month her birthday's in anyway."

Skyler wasn't sure whether that was Homer's attempt at a joke or not, but she still chuckled a little, because she found it funny. She figured that probably they had different ideas of what constituted something funny. Him with his rocket scientist's job, and her with her waitressing job at the diner.

"What about Saylor? I mean, you don't have to use it if you don't want to, but Saylor as in S-A-Y-L-O-R, it's kind of similar to Skyler, and she was born beside Lake Michigan, so... Maybe she'll be a sailor."

Skyler mulled that over in her head a little bit, liking it immediately but trying to look at it from every angle. Saylor, spelled a little differently, a little bit similar to her name.

"I like it. That was really good. Wow, you're actually really good at picking out names."

He grinned. "I know I'm not the father or anything, but everyone around here is kind of expecting me to be right now, so I guess I need to pull my weight in the naming category."

Her smile slipped just a little. "I really am sorry about that. I know that's not what you want."

He lifted his shoulder. "I really didn't mind. We know the truth, and if they think I am, it's not that big a deal." He grinned a little. "I did deliver her."

That was true, he did.

"And you named her. I'm going with Saylor. I don't think Saylor April sounds very good together, so we'll have to think of a new middle name." She narrowed her eyes at him and tilted her head. "Do you have any ideas in that direction?"

He'd done such a good job of picking a first name for her.

"What's your middle name?"

"Grace. But I don't know what it's for."

"What about Faith? Or Joy? Something to go along with Grace."

Saylor Faith. Saylor Joy.

"I like Saylor Faith. Actually, I like Saylor Grace. I suppose we could share the same middle name. What do you think? Saylor Grace?"

"I like it. It goes nice together."

"All right then. Saylor Grace Montgomery. Montgomery is my last name."

"Yeah. I guess I definitely wouldn't be giving her anyone else's name. Especially after what he...did." Homer's voice was pitched low, and it growled a little, sending something that felt warm and good down her backbone. She hadn't noticed his voice doing that before, but maybe it was the way he had pitched it, out of respect for her or maybe being careful of her feelings. It didn't matter, because she didn't really care.

She had been struggling to like Jeff anyway. She had stayed because she felt it was the right thing to do. She didn't want to hop from man to man to man, leaving one just because he wasn't exactly what she wanted him to be. Of course, Jeff was far from what she wanted, but she didn't want to be the kind of person who didn't stick with things. Even when they were hard.

But now that he left, she almost felt free, or would, if she didn't feel so scared.

"Yeah."

They sat there in silence for a few seconds with Skyler again wondering whether she should try to feed her baby.

She didn't have a chance to even think about it because just then the nurse walked in.

"Oh, look at this. This is the little darling that didn't want to wait to get to the hospital before she came into the world. What a sweetie," the nurse said, smiling as she walked over and looked at Saylor like she was the first baby she'd ever seen.

It made Skyler feel rather proud to have someone else oohing and aahing over her baby. She hadn't expected to feel that way. But she immediately liked the nurse for the sole reason that the nurse liked her baby. Crazy how parenting could change a person.

Now, apparently the only prerequisite she had to like someone was for them to like her child.

"Has Mama fed the baby yet?" the nurse asked as she pulled the blood pressure machine over to Skyler and started wrapping the band around her arm.

"No. She's... She's been sleeping since she was born."

"Here, you let Daddy hold her for a little bit, I'm going to finish taking your blood pressure."

She opened her mouth to say that Homer wasn't Daddy, but she remembered what he said about not minding being mistaken for the father, and she decided that there were too many other things to think about, and she would just let that one go.

Glancing at Homer, she thought he looked distinctly uncomfortable.

"If you don't want to—" she started to say, but he shook his head.

Before he could say anything, the nurse interjected. "Daddy needs to learn to hold the baby too. She needs both parents to take care of her."

That made Skyler rethink her attempt to inform the nurse that Homer was going above and beyond any roles that he absolutely had to play, but he cleared his throat, shuffled a little, and shifted his hands around, as though trying to figure out the very best way to put them underneath the child.

"I can't remember ever holding a baby before."

"Are you serious?" The nurse looked up as she released the air on the blood pressure cuff.

"Yeah. I... I just haven't."

"My goodness. You have to make sure you support her head, and oh, I didn't even notice that she's wrapped in a towel. Boy, she really was born at home. My goodness." The nurse chuckled a little and then went on to show Homer where to put his hands and how to support the head.

Skyler was a little fascinated at the way his big hands looked next to the tiny little baby. Even though all she could see of Saylor was her head.

But Homer was able to take her from the nurse and cradled her in the crook of his arm. He didn't look exactly comfortable, but he looked extremely adorable. Suddenly Skyler wished she had her phone so she could take a picture. Not that Homer was the dad, but...that was almost how it felt.

It would be a picture of the man who delivered the baby. But if wishes were horses, and all that, since she didn't have her phone and had no idea where it might be.

All her contacts were on the phone too, so she couldn't even get a hold of Jeff, even if she wanted to. She had no idea what his number was. It was programmed into her phone, and she'd never bothered to memorize it.

Ten

The nurse took her stethoscope and listened to Saylor's lungs, and then she said, "I need to go get a smaller blood pressure cuff for the baby. I think I'll have to steal it from the maternity floor, since we don't have any such thing around here. I'll be right back."

She left the room.

Skyler barely noticed. She was so enraptured looking at Homer holding Saylor. He looked down at the baby with a look of wonder on his face. One big hand was up, and he had a finger out, touching the tiny little fist that still nestled right beside her chubby little chin.

"She's so perfect," he murmured. "I didn't notice that when she was born."

"There was a lot going on at that time," Skyler said, not really wanting to think about that. It was...embarrassing, but also now that she saw Homer holding Saylor, there was something precious about it as well.

She loved the tender way he moved and the gentle way he cradled the baby, like she was the most precious thing in the world.

Again, it was those weird parenting things that were kicking in all of a sudden. Homer liked her baby, so she...liked Homer. Although, there was some weird feeling going on in her chest that took her by surprise.

It felt warm and big and deep, and she wasn't quite sure what to name it.

The nurse came back with the smaller blood pressure cuff, took the baby from Homer, and it was about that time that she realized the baby wasn't wearing a diaper.

Skyler would have laughed, but she was too busy trying to pay attention to how the nurse cleaned the baby up, since she had no idea how to do that.

Some newborn diapers soon found their way to the room, as well as some protection for Skyler, which she desperately needed.

The doctor came in, pronounced both of them healthy and strong, and said he could admit them if they wanted him to, but they seemed to be doing just fine, and they were free to go if that's what they preferred.

Skyler got the idea that the doctor thought that maybe they were homebirth kind of people who just came into the hospital to get checked out or something.

After he said that, he looked at Skyler like she could make the decision immediately.

She glanced at Homer, who lifted his brows and in a barely perceptible way shrugged his shoulders.

She wanted to ask if she chose to go home, which was her preference, would she be going home with him? Was he going to say okay and then walk out of the hospital and leave without her?

Forgive her, but she had been left before, and the idea of being left again didn't seem so outrageously ridiculous.

Deciding that it might be better to be homeless now than homeless tomorrow on top of owing the hospital for a night's stay, she gathered up her courage and said, "Thank you, but I prefer to not be admitted if it's possible. As long as you think Saylor's going to be all right."

"I do." He nodded his head decisively. "I can't let you go right away, the nurses are working on the birth certificate and Social Security form and that type of thing. They'll bring some paperwork in, and then, once you have all of that filled out, you'll be free to go."

It felt like the longest night of her life, and she realized that it probably was close to morning, and she hadn't had a wink of sleep. Of course, Homer hadn't, either.

After the doctor left, she pushed aside her tiredness and looked at Homer, who had settled himself in a chair, the baby in his arm.

She hesitated, not wanting to bring up the unpleasant subject when they were looking so cute together, but she said, "I wasn't sure where I was going to go if he allowed us to go right now. But I thought it would be better to leave without owing them for a night's stay."

"Well, technically, we actually have stayed the night, but beyond that, I assumed I was going to take you home. I couldn't leave you here. We can just assume that you'll stay for," he hesitated, then said, "two weeks." He sounded like he was making it up as he went along. "After that, we'll talk about it. Surely by then, the guy who left you will show up or something. And you were going to take some time off from your job anyway, right?"

"Yeah," she said, although she hadn't thought any such thing. She supposed she thought she was going to be back to work as soon as she could. Since the diner didn't exactly offer paid maternity leave. Or unpaid maternity leave. She would just be taking time off, and it would annoy her supervisor, but her supervisor could hardly require that she work when she was in the hospital.

"All right, unless you had something else in mind?" he asked softly.

"No. I didn't."

She looked away, but her gaze was brought back to Saylor and Homer as Saylor shifted, and then she went from contentedly sleeping to screaming at the top of her lungs in less time than it took Skyler to blink.

"Wow. That was unexpected," Homer said, straightening up from his casual pose and holding Saylor as though she was a bomb about to go off.

Skyler scooted off the hospital bed and, feeling very conscious of the big, gaping hole in the back of her gown, held her arms out to Homer as she walked toward the chair. "I can take her," she said, knowing that was what a mother was supposed to say but not knowing what in the world she was going to do with the baby when she did take her.

The nurse bustled in, and Skyler took a quick second to thank the Lord they weren't busy. "When we asked if you were bottle-feeding or breast-feeding, you said you were going to breast-feed, so this is a good time for you to get started and have a little practice. If you'd like, we have a lactation consultant on staff, and she can come in and give you some pointers."

The chipper nurse, way too happy for the hour of night it was, or rather hour of the morning, walked in with a clipboard full of papers in one hand and supplies for Skyler in the other.

"I... I don't know if I need any help or not, since I've never done it before."

"That's fine. You sit down on the bed, and we can figure it out."

"I... I think I'll go use the restroom," Homer said, unfolding himself from the chair, and Skyler was impressed that he didn't run as fast as he could out of the room.

"Now you just wait right there, Daddy. Mom is going to need your help, and you can't leave her when things get uncomfortable."

"Actually, Mama probably doesn't need your help," Skyler said, biting her lip and looking at the nurse, because she just couldn't bring herself to look at Homer.

"All right. Whatever," the nurse said, still a cheerful voice, but with an undertone to it loudly saying that she disagreed with some people's parenting choices.

Skyler, on the other hand, really appreciated Homer leaving. This was going to be awkward enough without him standing there "helping."

Maybe if he actually were the father, or yeah, if he were the father, it would be different. Although, she couldn't picture Jeff helping. But mostly because of Jeff, not because of any uncomfortableness she felt.

It wasn't as hard as what she feared it would be, and she found that both Saylor and she took to nursing rather naturally. She heard some horror stories from working in the diner, patrons who saw she was expecting and felt free to share their birth and nursing stories with her, so she'd heard the spectrum.

Thankful that at least one thing was going well for her, she only felt a twinge of nervousness when she thought that Homer might come back in before she was done.

"I'm sure you guys want to get home. You've been out all night, and you must be exhausted. So I took the liberty of filling these out for you, and mostly they just need your signatures. You can go through them at your leisure, and the birth certificate and Social Security form you can leave here at the hospital, and we'll send them in for you."

Skyler nodded, only half listening. She had fallen in love with her baby again and hadn't even realized such a feeling was possible. This overwhelming, deep, all-encompassing love that she felt for this little human who depended on her for everything.

Unfortunately for Saylor. Since Skyler was not equipped to provide even the basic necessities for herself, let alone a child.

She was depending on Homer, and it grated a little bit, but for now she really appreciated him.

She had heard, although she had never been able to put it into practice, that when a person was afraid, in order to take their fear and replace it with something else, they needed to take themselves, put their eyes on Jesus, and fill the place where they were afraid with Jesus.

She wasn't sure whether she could do that, wasn't sure whether she could give up control of her future, since she had no idea what she was going to do tomorrow, let alone any further in the future, but she tried to think about how Jesus loved her. And how he was kind and caring and compassionate and wouldn't want anything bad to happen to her.

It eased her anxiety somewhat, and as long as she didn't allow the thought of tomorrow in her head, she seemed to be all right.

It was at least a half an hour later before Homer came in. He carried two cups of coffee in his hand and a small package underneath his arm.

"The cafeteria is open. Did you realize it was seven o'clock in the morning?"

"No. I had no idea."

"Miss Vera is still with my mom. I just talked to them, and they're fine, but I feel like I need to hurry home. Are you ready?"

"Yeah. There are some papers there they said we needed to sign before being discharged, and I put my name everywhere I thought I was supposed to. I think there might be a couple for you to sign." She thought it had to do with billing and that type of thing, and she hated to make him pay for it, but it had been in his name. At least they had his name underneath the line where the signature was required.

"All right," Homer said in a preoccupied voice as he picked up the papers and skimmed through them.

She watched out of the corner of her eye as he hesitated over a couple and then, as though making up his mind, scribbled his name at the bottom. She really, really hoped she wasn't putting him out by having him put his name on the line saying that he was going to pay for her care.

"Did they give you anything to wear home?"

"Oh, yes. They had some clothes from the lost and found." They had also given her some disposable underwear, which was a godsend in her opinion, and she appreciated being able to be modest as she walked around the room.

"All right. You can get changed if you'd like and we can head out."

"Actually, I totally forgot, but you guys can't leave until you have a car seat." The nurse had come back in and spoke in a cheerful voice.

"Oh."

It was on the tip of Skyler's tongue to ask if they could just ride home carrying the baby, but they already rode there doing that, and it had made her nervous.

"Thankfully, I was able to get this from the donations that came in over the last week, which we haven't yet taken to our sister branch of Every Life Matters, where we typically take all the donations we're given." She held up an infant seat, still attached to the base.

"It even has instructions." She smiled ruefully. "They got a little more complicated than they were back when I had babies."

She laughed a little and handed the car seat to Homer who took it gingerly.

"All right. Sounds good. I appreciate it." He looked the car seat over, and then clicked the latch to detach it from the base, and figured out how to set it beside her on the hospital bed, putting the handle down and checking out the straps.

"Looks like they're already adjusted for the newborn size. I think she'll fit just fine in there."

"I also have a few outfits for Saylor. A couple of them are blue, but I figured beggars wouldn't be choosy, and of course you're welcome to take all of these diapers and the other things that are already here."

The nurse sighed, and then she came over, and without even pausing, she wrapped her arms around Skyler. Skyler found herself wanting to lean into her embrace, since she couldn't hug her back since Saylor was in her arms.

"You two are the cutest. It isn't every day that we get to have the kind of excitement that you guys brought here last night. I hope everything goes well for you. And maybe we'll see you again." She stood back, beaming down at Skyler like Skyler had done something wonderful, rather than have a baby in a garage and show up in the middle of the night at the emergency room.

"Thanks so much for everything." And Skyler meant it with all her heart, even if she didn't have the words to say it. Then, Homer took Saylor, and they tucked her in the car seat, using one of the warming blankets to cover her with. Skyler gathered up all of the things that they'd been given, and they walked out of the emergency room, a baby between them.

Eleven

Homer lifted the window in his study. He didn't used to like to work with the outside air coming in, but lately he'd begun to crave it. Maybe because he felt claustrophobic.

Or maybe... He wasn't sure why else. He just... Maybe he needed a change. He wasn't sure. Maybe it was because of the disorder that seemed to have permeated his life.

It used to be that he focused on his work and that was all he had, and then his mom got worse and worse and he had to focus on that, but he didn't mind because he loved her.

But yesterday had completely upended his life, and he wasn't sure... what to do about it.

On the one hand, he knew as a human, he could hardly kick Skyler out on her rear. After all, humans couldn't treat other humans that way. He had to do the very best that he could, and he had. He delivered a baby, despite the fact that he knew nothing about them, had taken her to the hospital, signed the dotted line saying that he would pay whatever charges were incurred, and...did a little more than that.

Maybe that's what he was wondering about. He wasn't sure if he had done the right thing.

And he also wasn't sure where to go from there. He'd been walking on pins and needles all day because after Skyler and Saylor had come home from the hospital, they had gone into the living room and lain down on the couch and he hadn't heard a sound from either one of them.

Either Saylor was the best baby ever, or babies didn't cry nearly as much as what he had been led to believe.

What was he going to do with them? What was he going to do about what he did in the hospital?

He sat back down and pressed his fingers together, forming a steeple with them, elbows on the desk, his chin resting on his thumbs, his pointer fingers resting on his nose.

It was a good position in which to think, but no answers were coming to him.

He didn't want additional responsibilities in his house and didn't want a mom and her baby living there either.

But he liked Skyler. She hadn't taken anything for granted and on the way home had even said that if he kept track of what she owed him, she would try to pay him back. It would come slowly, she said. But she'd do it.

He didn't want to take her money. She didn't even have any money.

And that wasn't necessarily the problem. He had been blessed to be born to parents who could afford pretty much anything he wanted, and he had worked hard and got an education and gotten a good job and could still afford pretty much anything he wanted.

He didn't want much, just some peace and quiet and a place to work. He liked that he didn't have to go to an office, and he appreciated the fact that he could take care of his mother.

He wasn't blind to the fact that his days with his mom were limited. Especially the days where his mom knew who he was.

There had been an idea that had been percolating in the back of his head, curling there for a while. But he didn't know whether he wanted to bring it out and examine it. After all, he barely knew Skyler. He didn't know whether he wanted her living in his house or not, and he definitely didn't know whether he wanted her taking care of his mom, but the idea was there. She could be a caregiver.

He could pay her, she could stay, she would have a place for the baby, she would have a place to live, and he would have someone he could depend on making sure his mother didn't do anything to hurt herself and wouldn't burn the house down.

It might only be a temporary measure. He might not be able to keep her in her home as was her wish. But he would do his best.

And Skyler just might be able to help him with it.

Realizing it was almost lunchtime, he took one more glance out the window where his mother moved among the garden. It used to be a beautiful place to sit and ponder but had grown up in weeds since the disease had started taking over. Days like today, she would go out and sometimes sit, sometimes work, but she didn't seem to have the mental capacity that it took to make it look the way it did back in its glory days.

He didn't care how the garden looked, and he let her do whatever she wanted to with it.

Maybe he should offer to help. But it was almost noon and time to get started on something to eat for lunch. He supposed that if Skyler was up, he could propose his idea to her, although maybe he would want to do a background check. She didn't have any documents, but surely she had her Social Security number memorized. He had to be able to figure out how to run that through at least police records and a child welfare database as well.

He went downstairs quietly, just in case Skyler was still sleeping.

He saw he still had enough chicken breast to make a meal for everyone, and there was Dr Pepper in the refrigerator as well.

It looked like he'd be making more Dr Pepper chicken, and he couldn't say that he minded. It was one of his mother's favorites, and if Skyler had even a little bit of a sweet tooth, she would enjoy it as well.

He prepped the food and put it in the oven, and then as though drawn by a pull he couldn't explain, his feet took him across the hall until he was standing at the entrance to the living room, his eyes landing first on the baby nestled beside Skyler partially on her stomach, partially against the back of the couch. She lay on her back, and her hand absently stroked along the baby's back.

Thankfully they were both decently clothed.

But as his eyes moved upward, he realized she was looking at him.

"How are you feeling?" he asked, trying to pretend he was there to check on her. That wasn't exactly why he had come, but he couldn't put his finger on any other reason.

"Sore."

"After what I saw yesterday, it's hard to imagine you do not have extreme pain. I was surprised you were able to walk." Maybe he was being too honest, but that was his assessment. Even seeing the size of the baby now, it was hard to imagine it came out of something as small as Skyler. There wasn't much to her.

He guessed it was probably because she didn't have a lot of money to buy food, but maybe she was just built small.

"Not extreme pain. But...definitely uncomfortable. Pretty much anywhere a person can feel pain, I think I feel it."

He narrowed his eyes. "Did I hear the nurse telling you about certain medication you could take that wouldn't affect the baby?"

"Basically Tylenol. I think Robitussin maybe for coughing, but for pain, I'm limited to Tylenol."

"I'll get you some."

"I wasn't asking you to," she said quickly, shifting a little, like she planned to get up and run after him.

"You stay there. I'll be back with some Tylenol." He waited until she settled down, his eyes keeping hold of hers.

He didn't know why he wanted to make sure that she understood that she wasn't to move. Normally he didn't go around thinking that he was a nursemaid. In fact, he couldn't remember taking care of anyone except for his mother, and that had been a learning experience. Even now, it was a learning experience.

He grabbed the Tylenol and a glass of water, wondering about the sweet tea that his mother had spilled on the floor. Did Skyler drink sweet tea?

He wasn't sure, but he figured water would do to get the Tylenol down, and they could figure out the details later. He took it in, handing it to her as she murmured a thank you then tried to adjust herself so she could take the pills and drink the water.

"I don't have a straw, sorry."

"Okay. I... It hurts to move, and I don't want to wake her up. I was hoping to keep her quiet so she didn't bother you."

"I can pick her up, but that might wake her."

"If you don't mind?" She looked at him, and he appreciated the fact that she was trying to make things easier for him. Maybe because she was afraid that he would kick her out of his house. He shoved the thought aside. Maybe it was because that was the way she was, considerate to other people.

He didn't answer, but reached down, and thought about how the nurse told him to hold the baby while he struggled to get his hands under her without touching Skyler any more than what he had to. He wasn't sure why that was so important, but it seemed like it was and made things a little bit harder, but finally he had picked Saylor up and held her cradled in his arm.

Looking at her little face, as her eyes blinked open and her nose wrinkled up, gave him the same feeling that he had yesterday when he was looking at her. He hadn't been expecting it, but something warm and soft curled around his heart. Maybe that was the way everyone felt when they looked at a little baby.

He'd never seen one this young, certainly never held one. Perhaps all babies had the same effect on everyone. Any baby might have had the effect on him.

As he looked down, he could easily see Skyler's nose and the curve of her forehead. There was so much of Saylor's mother on Saylor's face that it was impossible not to tell that Skyler was her mom. Maybe it was because he had delivered the baby. Maybe that was why his heart felt gripped in that strength of love and warmth.

Or maybe it was because Saylor was just an exceptionally cute baby. She blinked her little eyes up and seemed to look right at him, even though he could tell she wasn't focusing. Her little body stretched, even though her legs must have stayed curled up next to her stomach, and he vaguely remembered the nurse talking about swaddling and how babies felt safer when they were tightly wrapped in a blanket, since it mimicked the feeling of being in the womb. Her back arched, and her little fists moved, until she relaxed and settled back in his arms, her fist going back by her face, her hand stretching.

He couldn't remember ever seeing anything more beautiful, more amazing,

Vaguely he realized Skyler had shifted, taking the pills and downing water.

"Do you mind holding her while I use the restroom?" she asked, sounding tentative as she pushed to a sitting position on the couch.

"Yeah. Go right ahead. I... I have some chicken in the oven for lunch, but I wanted to talk to you first if you can."

"All right," she said, sounding a little scared but resolved.

He tore his eyes from Saylor long enough to walk to the window where he could see his mom still happily puttering in the garden. The gate was shut, but of course she could unlock it at any time. He remembered that he had wanted to call someone to put locks on the doors so they would take a code to unlock or something. Something to keep her in so that she couldn't leave without someone knowing. Even if Skyler were to help him watch her, she couldn't do it twenty-four seven, and she couldn't possibly be expected to know where his mother was in the middle of the night.

He had promised his mother he wouldn't send her away from her home, and he was going to try to keep that promise. If there was any human way possible.

"I can take her back now, if you want me to." Skyler had come back and stood in the living room, not too close to him but close enough that he could hand the baby over.

"I'm okay holding her if you want a break." He probably should have handed her back. He wasn't comfortable with babies and had no idea why he really wanted to hold this one.

"Actually, here." He handed her over.

Skyler took her back without comment.

Homer walked to the end of the room and stood looking at the big window that opened out into the street. His mother had lace curtains in front of it, which he supposed went well with the thick walnut trim, old-fashioned and way too expensive to put in a new home today. But when this house was built, no expense was spared. The tile floor was a light yellow, and the walls were bluish gray.

The whole room felt warm and inviting yet somehow spacious and bright as well.

No wonder his mother didn't want to leave. And he was going to invite a stranger to live with them.

"Do you know your Social Security number?"

"I do," Skyler said, but her mouth closed and she didn't offer it to him.

It was just as well. He didn't have his phone out to take it down, although he could probably remember it. He was kind of good at that type of thing.

"Do you have any idea what you're planning on doing next?"

"I can be out of here. Today if that's what you want," she said immediately. She could barely walk, it was all she could do to go to the bathroom, and she was in pain, he could see it from the way she gingerly sat down and shifted to the side as though trying to find a spot where she could sit and it didn't hurt.

"Don't be ridiculous."

Maybe he should have said that a little bit more gently.

"I'm not. I don't expect you to keep me forever. I told you that yesterday. If you need me out, I'll leave."

"No. Actually...I was going to ask you to stay."

She didn't say anything. But her eyes flew to his as her mouth hung open. He almost told her not to drop the baby, but her mothering instincts must have kicked in, because her arms did not relax at all.

"I couldn't just move in here."

He wanted to point out that she basically already had. Pretty much everything she owned was in his house.

Of course, he didn't know what she had back in Chicago. Maybe she did have an apartment full of things that she was just itching to get back to.

Maybe he should ask about that.

"I guess I never even thought to offer you a ride back to your apartment in Chicago. I could do that."

"All right. I probably won't stay there. I shared it with Jeff."

Yeah. He figured. For some reason, that rubbed him the wrong way. Other than the fact that his mother would have died if he would have told her that he was living with anyone without being married to them.

"We were engaged," she said, as though she could read his thoughts on his face. He thought he was being more impassive than that. "I thought he meant forever. I...made a mistake."

"Regardless, you've noticed that my mother has Alzheimer's." He thought about trying to lead into his request, beat around the bush a little, but direct had always been his way. So he said, "I've been thinking for a while that I needed to hire someone to take care of her. I asked about your Social Security number because I want to run it, just to make sure."

"I don't have a record."

"Just to make sure, and then, if you're interested, I can figure out what the going rate is for adult day care and pay you accordingly."

"I don't know if I would be able to find a place to stay."

"Food and board would be included in your salary. There are four bedrooms upstairs we're not using, plus a sitting room that could easily double as the baby's room, since it's connected to two of the bedrooms. I might be getting a little ahead of myself. I need your Social Security number first."

He kept reminding himself he had to check her out and make sure. He couldn't just pretend that he liked her so therefore she was an acceptable type of person to have around his mother.

"Of course. Would you like to write it down?"

"Go ahead and give it to me." He looked at his watch. "I have a few minutes before the chicken comes out of the oven. I'll run upstairs and write it down up there, and see if I can run it in a few places. I've never done such a thing, so it might take a little bit to figure out the ropes."

She nodded, and he assumed she probably had never run anyone's Social Security number either. It wasn't something a normal person had to do. He might have to check out the tax implications too. So he made a mental note to contact his accountant and see exactly what he needed to do in order to have Skyler on payroll. He couldn't imagine that it would be easy.

She rattled the number off, and he saw the pattern right away, telling her he would be back down as he went upstairs. Well, that was the first step. If her number checked out okay, he would be asking her to stay. It was an odd thought. But somehow, it was a good one too.

Twelve

Two days after Saylor was born, Skyler felt more sore than she had just after delivery. Maybe endorphins or something had numbed the pain, or maybe exhaustion made it worse. Since Saylor slept almost all day long, and she was up pretty much all night every night.

Homer had taken her Social Security number but had not told her what the results were. She supposed those things took time.

She lived on Tylenol and had to force herself to eat so that she would be able to make milk for the baby.

She didn't have much of an appetite, and honestly, she was exhausted. But the idea of being able to stay, here, in this house, with her baby, was so amazing, she had to ask herself over and over again if she was dreaming or if it was really real.

Homer seemed to be watching his mom closely, and earlier that day, men had come to put locks on the doors. Homer had given her the codes and told her that no matter what she did, she should not allow his mother to have the codes. In other words, if his mother wanted to go out of the house, she needed to tell either him or her, but she could not go on her own.

Skyler hoped she was strong enough to stand up to his mom and not give in.

So far, the little bit that she had seen of Homer's mother made her seem like a nice, gentle lady, who was sweet, if not a little baffled with everything.

"Why, good morning, Linda," Gertie said from the doorway.

She had called Skyler Linda since that first day that she had come in to use the restroom.

"And I see you've had the baby already."

She'd said that every morning so far. "Yeah. A little girl."

"A girl?" She seemed confused. "I thought it was a boy."

"No. A girl. Your son suggested Saylor as a name, and I loved it. What do you think?"

"My son?" Gertie said, her brows going way up.

"Yeah. Homer said I should call her Saylor, which is very close to Skyler, which is my name."

"Your name is Linda," Homer's mother said from the doorway, and she didn't sound quite as nice. A little bit more strident, like she was losing her temper or something.

Skyler didn't want to have an argument about it, so she said, "I'm sorry. You're right. What's your name?"

"Oh, Linda. Don't be silly. You know my name is Gertie."

"Of course. I'm sorry. I'm so silly today."

"You are being goofy. After all, I know your baby is a boy. I changed his diapers."

She really didn't want to allow Gertie to change Saylor's diapers, especially if Gertie was going to insist that Saylor was a boy. But Gertie seemed to be thinking about something back in the recesses of her mind. Perhaps something that happened years before between her and Linda. Maybe Linda really had had a boy.

"I'm glad that you're all settled in. Have you decided about giving the baby away?"

"No. I am not giving the baby away." Not if she could help it. She didn't know how someone could give their child away, although if it was the best decision for her baby, she'd do it in a heartbeat.

"Oh. Phil said you might."

Skyler racked her brain, trying to figure out who in the world Phil was. Did she know Phil? She made a mental note to ask Homer if he knew Phil. And Linda while she was at it. If she was going to be Linda, she ought to know who she was impersonating.

"I guess Phil knows what he is talking about." She wanted to get out of this conversation where she had no clue who the people were or what they did. She thought of the first thing she could. "I saw you out in the garden this morning."

"Yes," Gertie said, her face lighting up with a smile. "That's my happy place."

"Maybe you can teach me how to garden."

"I would like to do that. Maybe we can go out later today."

"Maybe not today. I'm still a little sore."

"Oh, I imagine you probably are. After everything you've been through. That's so sad."

"Yeah," Skyler agreed, unsure exactly what Gertie was talking about unless she truly knew that she had given birth in the garage.

"There's a pretty garden at the end of the road. Vera and Dominic came and created it in memory of their son. They asked me for my advice for them, things that grow well here in our little ecosystem. You know, even though we're in Michigan, and right beside the lake, there's little pockets of places that have their own weather, and different things grow well in different areas. I was flattered that they asked me. Vera is a world-class designer, you know."

"I didn't know. But that's interesting. I'd like to see the garden."

"We'll definitely have to go see it. I'm part of the group of ladies who take care of it. We all keep up with the garden and make sure that it's a beautiful place for anyone who wants to sit a spell. That's what I've always done with my garden. That, and grow vegetables to feed my family. After all, a woman who can be frugal with her husband's money is a jewel in his chest."

Skyler had never heard such a statement, and she wondered if maybe Gertie was getting her metaphors mixed up or something. Or maybe her old-fashioned sayings were as jumbled in her brain as some of the other things were.

"I better be going. Maybe when you feel better, we can go out and see my garden. And then, when the baby's big enough, we'll take a walk down the street."

"That sounds good, Miss Gertie."

"Linda. Why are you calling me Miss Gertie? Like I'm older than you are or something."

"I'm sorry."

The lady left, and Skyler sat on the couch, looking around at the bright, cheerful room where Gertie had held court for so many years. She loved her house and had asked to not have to leave it, but it seemed silly, since she mostly didn't even know where she was. Skyler couldn't tell which parts of the conversation were real and which parts weren't.

"Hey, I didn't know if you had a chance to go upstairs and pick out a room?" Homer came to the doorway, holding several packages in his hand. She hadn't even heard him come in from outside. He had said earlier that he was going to the store and had asked if she wanted anything. She'd asked for diapers and told him to take it out of her first check.

He told her that he wasn't even going to consider allowing her to start working until the baby was four weeks old, but she had told him that she would keep an eye on his mother while he was gone so he didn't have to take her. He appreciated that since he said it would make the trip shorter. And he didn't want it to take all morning. But he had some necessities he needed to get.

It looked like his "necessities" were sets of sheets.

"No. I'm sorry." The idea of climbing the stairs had made her want to groan. She was way too sore to even consider doing such a thing. But if he wanted her to pick out a room, she would climb the stairs.

Unless... "You can pick out a room and just give it to me. I don't really care. Although you'd mentioned there were two rooms that adjoined the sitting room, and I wouldn't mind having one of those."

"Are you sure you don't want to check? I have one of the bedrooms that opens to the sitting room. I'm fine with that. You'd have the room on the other side, but I just want to make sure you know. My study would actually be on the other side of your bedroom then."

"All right. I just appreciate you allowing me to stay and giving me a room. I'm not going to be picky about it." She took a breath. "But I will take those sheets and make the beds if you want me to."

"Don't be ridiculous."

That seemed to be his favorite saying. She smiled a little, and his serious face studied hers for just a bit before he grinned.

"When I say that, I feel like I'm being a little hard on you, so it's funny that it makes you laugh."

"I think it's one of your favorite sayings. Ridiculous must be an important word for you."

"I guess I do use it a lot. I...live with my mom, so my vocabulary can't be as colorful as maybe some other man's my age. Not that I want to use those words. I mostly don't."

She nodded and thought about that. She didn't typically like to use colorful language as he said. But it was mostly because she could hardly use it whenever she was taking orders at the restaurant. Customers did not appreciate waitresses who used a lot of profanity. And she was sure it would keep her from getting good tips.

Regardless, he took another long look at her that made her feel seen clear down to her bones, then nodded his head and turned and walked away.

Thirteen

Homer walked down to the one store in Raspberry Ridge. He wasn't sure if it would be open, since it wasn't tourist season, and Fran Holloway, who owned the store, wasn't exactly diligent about her hours.

Not that Homer typically cared. But he needed a blanket for the crib he bought for Saylor.

He shook his head as he walked down the street. He wasn't quite sure why he bought a crib. Or sheets, or blankets, or anything else. But... he had.

He'd also arranged with his boss to have two weeks off. He hardly ever took vacation time, and it was a good time since he was between projects, and he had so much vacation time backed up he could almost be off for an entire year without having to work at all.

He just never went anywhere. Other than to his mother's doctor's appointments, which he could typically schedule his day around.

Regardless, he wasn't quite sure why he used some of his vacation on a woman he didn't even know and her newborn baby, as cute as she was.

Bells jingled over his head as he walked in, and he had to duck a little so that the hanging golden balls didn't hit him on the forehead.

Fran looked up as he walked in. Her eyes widened.

He had come in once or twice with his mother, but he never came in by himself. She seemed to look around him, leaning far to the left before her brows furrowed down.

"Is your mother ill?" she asked, and he doubted she meant to say it quite like that.

"She's doing as well as can be expected," he said casually, like she wasn't justified in her concern.

He almost smiled when she said, "But...you never come in by yourself. Is there a problem?"

"No. No problem." She was going to know exactly what was going on as soon as he picked up a baby blanket. He was kind of surprised she didn't already know. He might keep to himself a lot, but Raspberry Ridge was still a small town.

As he walked to the small display of baby items, Fran's expression went from shocked to knowing.

"I had heard that you were giving that girl a place to live. But I did not believe it. I said that kid has a level head on his shoulders and he is not going to hire someone that he does not know. And you just proved me wrong."

"Maybe I did," he said easily. Fran really was a nice lady. She had been very kind to his mother as she'd gotten less and less coherent. He liked her, really. And he supposed her shock and surprise and maybe a little bit of censure was just because she liked him and wanted the best for him. Maybe she was concerned about him.

"So... I heard that you were the father. Is that the truth?"

He thought again about what he did in the hospital. He supposed there was a subset of people who would say that he was not lying if he said yes. Technically, in the eyes of the state, he was.

"I delivered her."

"I know. In your garage. In a thunder and lightning storm, the worst one we've seen here in years." The woman seemed to think it was pertinent that those three things went together. As for Homer, he wasn't so sure.

"That's all true," he said simply, hoping that she forgot her question about him being the father. He needed to talk to Skyler at some point.

But he wasn't sure how to bring up what he wanted to discuss without her feeling bad.

He ran his hand over a couple of blankets. They felt a little scratchy and not good enough for Saylor. But after he pulled a couple off the top of the pile, he found a green one that felt silky, like velvet under his hand, and he knew he found exactly what he was looking for.

Then he wondered if maybe he should get two. Michigan summers were hot, but it could cool off pretty good in the evening. Maybe she'd get her blanket dirty if she were outside, and she'd need a clean one.

Seeing a purple one that was made out of the same material as the green, he pulled them both out of the pile, and his eye caught on a little stroller, one of those ones that folded up like an umbrella. Maybe they were called umbrella strollers. He seemed to recall hearing that term somewhere. And it would make sense.

He reached out and grabbed a hold of it. As far as he knew, Skyler didn't have any baby paraphernalia. She seemed content carrying the baby everywhere, setting her down when she had to, but eventually she would probably want to take walks and that type of thing, and a stroller would make it easier for her to keep an eye on his mother outside.

He justified the purchase to himself, even as he knew he was doing it just because...he wasn't even sure. But it wasn't to make Skyler's life easier or to help her with watching his mother.

His mother had nothing to do with it, if he was being honest. It was all about Skyler.

He put the two blankets and the stroller on the counter and resisted the urge to look over the front baby carrier that he saw behind the stroller container.

She could carry the baby snuggled up to her chest. In fact, the name even suggested snuggling.

"Is this it?" Fran said.

"Yes, ma'am. For now." He shifted from one foot to the other, a little uncomfortable. He didn't really like going out in public and never knew exactly what to say to people. Even though he considered Fran a friend. At least, a friend of his mother.

"How's your mom doing? I haven't seen her around lately. The last time I did, she called me Karen."

"Yeah. She's in good health, but sometimes she doesn't know who I am, and those times are becoming more frequent."

"She always begged me to make sure that you didn't take her to a home of any kind. I told her sometimes it was safer there. Maybe you would be wise to consider it, considering that she could get out not knowing who she is or able to tell someone how to get back to her house."

"I think pretty much everybody in Raspberry Ridge knows my mom."

"That's true. Although, ever since the church closed several years ago, Raspberry Ridge just doesn't seem the same."

Homer did actually miss the church. He wasn't one for going out a whole lot, but he always appreciated the Sunday morning sermons. They were like a shot in the arm. And Sunday night Bible study was like taking vitamins. Learning about Scripture never seemed to get old for him.

Although, since the church closed, he had to admit that he hadn't really started going anywhere else. His mom had said that she was too old to find a new church and try to fit into a new church family. It was like trying to fit into somebody else's family. Sometimes things just didn't quite line up.

"I know your mother isn't quite the same, but if she wants to join the ladies who take care of the garden this year, you know she's welcome."

"I believe she's planning on it. Skyler might be going with her."

"The new woman? And the baby?"

"Yeah." He hesitated. How much gossip did he want going around town?

And then he figured it was something that people were going to figure out eventually.

"I've hired her to take care of my mom while I work. So I would imagine she will go with my mom wherever she goes. And I know that you're going to make her feel like a part of the community. She...doesn't have much family." He hoped he wasn't saying more than Skyler wanted the town to know. But he had a feeling that if Fran knew that Skyler was in need, Fran would rise to the occasion. Fran was just the kind of woman who saw a need and loved to fulfill it. She probably was a little bit at loose ends since the church closed.

"All right, I'll keep that in mind. In fact, if you give me her number, maybe I'll just give her a ring later today and drop by with a little housewarming gift for the baby."

"She doesn't have a phone. Yet. It...got lost the day she had the baby. There were a lot of things going on."

"A phone is a rather important thing to lose," Fran said with her brows raised.

She did not make Homer feel guilty though. What he said was the honest-to-goodness truth. Her phone had gotten lost that day. She had no clue where it was, and it had left along with her boyfriend, her fiancé, or whoever the loser was who dropped her off and didn't pick her up again.

He got a little mad every time he thought about it. He wasn't exactly the best at thinking about people or getting along with them, but he would never leave his supposed girlfriend, his fiancée, especially if she were expecting his baby, along the side of the road. No matter how quaint the town seemed.

Fran put his blankets in a bag, and he carried the stroller in his hand.

"Thanks a lot. I'm sure Skyler will enjoy meeting you," he said, smiling to let her know that that wasn't a threat, although...he felt it was pretty important that Fran know that he expected her to be nice, inclusive, and kind.

"I'll enjoy meeting her as well. I'm sure Raspberry Ridge has room for one more, and the baby. It's been a while since we've had a baby around here." She nodded at him as he turned to leave. "Have a nice day."

He smiled and nodded his head. "Same to you."

That wasn't so bad. Mingling with the folks of Raspberry Ridge always left him feeling good, even though the idea of mingling with people was never something he looked forward to. Still, he felt like this was for Skyler and the baby, and maybe he just paved the way to make it a little easier for her to fit in their small town.

Fourteen

S he couldn't find any words.

Skyler ran her hands over the soft blanket that lay in the bottom of the crib that Homer had set up in what used to be the sitting room upstairs.

He had asked her to come up and tell him if everything was okay.

She wasn't sure why she needed to go up and look at bedsheets and had been extremely surprised when she had walked in and there was a brand-new crib set up with sheets and two ultrasoft blankets.

"I hope they're soft enough for her. The other blankets felt a little scratchy to me."

Homer sounded slightly uneasy, and he shifted from one foot to the other. That was the tell that he was nervous. She'd figured that out in the few days that she had spent in his house.

He'd taken to coming down in the evening and sitting in the living room with her.

She'd gotten good at nursing Saylor underneath the blanket, even though the ones that she got from the hospital were about the size of a quilting patch.

Still, it offered her some privacy, enough that Homer didn't seem uncomfortable.

She definitely hated making him uncomfortable.

But this, this was far more than she had even dreamed about. She had priced cribs back when she had first gotten pregnant and had hoped that the shower that Kylie had said she was going to throw would perhaps negate the need for her to purchase one.

For the last few days, Saylor had been sleeping on the couch with her. Skyler had been carefully lying on her back and not allowing herself to move. She didn't want to accidentally roll over on her baby.

Needless to say, she hadn't been getting very good rest. She assumed that whatever the bed looked like upstairs, Saylor would be sharing it with her. But this... This was...

"If you don't like it, we can take it back. I mean, I have the e-receipt and it's filed under Saylor in my inbox."

Her eyes flew to Homer.

And she still was speechless. Of course he'd had them email him the receipt. He seemed like the kind of person who nailed down every single thing, and of course he had a filing system for his inbox. Unlike hers, which was a jumbled mess of everything. But...the fact that he had a file named Saylor?

On top of that, he had spent hundreds of dollars on a crib.

"I love it," she finally managed to say, pushing the words out.

"You don't sound like you love it." Homer shifted, and then he ran a hand through his hair. "This was stupid. I'm sorry. I don't know why I even—" He broke off abruptly, turning on his toe and pushing out of the room.

"Please. Wait!" She wasn't quite as sore as she had been, and she hurried to him, putting a hand on his arm as he made it to the doorway of the room.

He didn't look at her.

He ran a hand through his hair again, shoving that hand in his pocket, although the arm that her hand rested on did not move.

"I just...wanted to do something nice."

"This is... This is nicer than anything I could have imagined. I was having trouble finding words to tell you how amazing it was. I didn't even have a crib at home. They were too expensive. I never dreamed of having one this beautiful. It is a crib fit for a princess."

"Saylor is a little princess." He looked a little embarrassed that he said it, but his jaw jutted out like he wasn't going to take it back, and she couldn't make him.

She wouldn't dream of trying to make him take it back. His words made her smile, but she was careful not to laugh. He was sensitive about it. Obviously.

"Please. Come back. I will try to find the words. The blanket is so soft. I've never felt a blanket that soft, and the gift is so thoughtful. I wasn't expecting this. You've already done so much for me."

He put a hand up. "Stop. I haven't done that much. You don't have to bring it up every time we talk."

He sounded a little gruff, but she smiled anyway. She didn't think he really meant it. After all, he just bought her daughter a crib and two blankets, plus he'd put it together himself, and somehow, he managed to do it without her even noticing.

Obviously, the man had a big heart. Not that she thought that money and gifts meant everything, but it was the time he took to order it, get it, and set it up. The fact that he even thought about it in the first place. That he'd seen a need, and he even mentioned the softness of the blankets. It was...so much. She was tempted to put her arms around him and give him a hug. Just a "thank you so much for being so kind to me" kind of hug. But she thought that might make him uncomfortable as well. He didn't seem like he was much of a hugger.

"You have," she insisted.

His head turned toward her just a little bit. "Really?"

She nodded. "Really. I... Your generosity is overwhelming. Honestly, I'm not used to people being this nice to me. I don't recall ever in my life having anyone be this nice. And I can't help but feel a little bit like I don't deserve it."

"You've been getting along well with my mother. She talks about you when you're not around. Which is odd. Sometimes she doesn't remember your name, sometimes she calls you Linda. But she always smiles when she's talking about you. You managed to find a way to get past the blurriness of her disease, for lack of a better way to describe it, and become someone she trusts and likes."

"I don't know why. Maybe it's the magic of having a baby. She does love my baby, although she keeps insisting it's a boy."

"Yeah, I've heard her. I'm not sure why."

Skyler was starting to have some suspicions, but she kept them to herself for now. She thought that maybe there was some information about Homer's past that perhaps he didn't know. Or maybe he didn't talk about. She wasn't sure which.

She put a little pressure on the arm she was holding, trying to turn him toward her, and he didn't resist but allowed her to turn him to face her.

"Thank you. Thank you from the bottom of my heart, thank you. I feel like it was too much, but I appreciate you thinking of us and getting it, putting it together, and surprising me with it." She laughed a little. "I can't remember the last time I had a surprise this good."

That was easy. Never. She'd never had a surprise as good. She didn't really remember too much about birthdays or Christmases, and if her foster family did celebrate, it wasn't something that made her feel special and loved. Not like this. She always felt like they did it because they had to. Maybe that wasn't what they meant, but it was how it made her feel.

"Are you going to set her down and see how she likes it?"

"Yes, and I'd like to wrap her up in the blanket too. It's so soft."

"Yeah. I thought of her as soon as I felt it. And I got her two. I thought if you got one dirty, she'd have a different one to use."

"Maybe one of these will end up being her blankie. Some kids have one."

"I hadn't thought about that. Maybe."

They walked over to the edge of the crib, and she hesitated before she shifted Saylor out of the crook of her arm and held her out to Homer. "Would you like to do the honors?"

He looked at her, then looked at the baby, and the look on his face was serious.

"Yeah. I would." He sounded like he was surprised.

"That's only right, since you got it for her."

"It's yours. Forever. I...obviously have no need for a crib, but if you...need to go. It can go with you."

He was stumbling a little, but she understood what he was saying, ensuring that she didn't feel like this was something she had to return or something she was only getting the use of, but it was actually hers to keep.

"Even if Jeff came back, I wouldn't go with him. If that's what you're asking. I mean, as long as I can stay here."

"Of course you can. I wasn't sure how you felt about that. You... seem a little down, but it might be because of the pain and exhaustion."

"Yeah. I was just thinking about how I hadn't been getting any sleep because I'm keeping Saylor on me while I sleep, and this crib will be a godsend."

"If she sleeps."

"She seems to be the kind of baby that isn't real fussy. Which I really appreciate. Seems like so many times in my life, God has given me the hard part. He gave most of the easy parts away. But I guess I get to keep that easy part."

"So you do believe in God?" he asked, holding Saylor to him, cuddling her a little, like he wanted to hug her before he put her in the crib.

"You know, I guess I had some teaching here and there as I grew up. And sometimes I think that it's God's job just to be mean to me. You know?"

"I can see how you think that."

He didn't say anything more, and she felt a little bit at a loss as to what to do with her hands. It was funny—she'd only had a baby for a few days, and already she was used to constantly having a child in her arms.

"But I don't know. I know that that's not always the way He's presented. And I'd like to believe there is some goodness and light in there."

"My mom has a full collection of scriptural books. If... If you want to, you're welcome to come into my study anytime and read. Of course you can take the books with you, but there are several comfortable chairs, and sometimes Mom would sit in there while I worked. And just read her books. It was...companionable."

"Oh. Maybe I'll do that. Sometime if Saylor and your mom take a nap at the same time, I might come in. Thank you. I feel like I probably need to learn a little more. If I'm going to raise my daughter to believe in God, I ought to know what to teach her."

"That's right. You should."

"Your mom always talks about having Bible study. She must have really enjoyed studying the Word when she was younger."

"She did. She brought me up that way. Dad... He was a little different."

She didn't say anything, because she'd been wondering if there might be reasons why his dad wasn't around anymore. But she didn't want to say anything. So she just let it go.

"Thank you for the invitation, and thank you again for the crib."

He leaned over and carefully set Saylor down in it.

"I think she likes it," he said.

"Oh, I can tell she does."

He took one of the blankets and carefully set it over Saylor as she lay there swaddled in the blankets from the hospital.

"Do you mind if I take a picture?"

"Not at all. I really miss my phone for that reason. Figures, the first time in my life I have something I really want to take pictures of, and I don't have a phone."

"That reminds me. I ordered one from the Internet. It should be here this afternoon."

"You didn't."

How was she ever going to pay him back?

"I can see you wondering how you're ever going to pay me back."

"How did you know?"

"Because it's what you always say. You don't have to pay me back. You need to have a phone if you're going to be watching my mom. It's part of your job. Although, it's yours to keep."

"I feel like I keep thanking you, because you keep showering me with all these things I don't deserve."

"Maybe you do deserve them. Don't sell yourself short."

They stood there, standing at the edge of the crib, her looking up into his eyes, and him looking down. Something seemed to pass between them, and she wasn't quite sure what it was. But it felt...safe. *Safe.*

Fifteen

"I think the ladies who tend the flowers should have a bigger goal." Fran sat on Vera's porch, sipping a cold glass of iced tea, enjoying the warmth of the sunny Michigan day, cooled gently by the lake breeze that blew in. Just the perfect temperature to keep the day from being too hot.

May days were not always this nice, but a person needed to enjoy them while they had them.

"I can't disagree with that. What kind of bigger goal were you thinking about?" Vera asked, looking sleek and chic as usual in blue tailored trousers, with a breezy white flowing shirt that had enough buttons unbuttoned to see the blue shirt she wore under it. Her hair was softly tied back, with strands of it escaping to blow around her face, and the bracelets on her wrist jingled as she set her tea back down on the table.

She always looked cool, calm, and collected. Fran had never seen her looking otherwise, although surely she had.

Rumor in town had it that she and her husband had been estranged until they had come back to Raspberry Ridge together to make a garden in memory of their son.

Fran knew Vera years ago when she had grown up in Raspberry

Ridge, but she'd been busy with her career and hadn't been around much for the last decade.

Fran for one was happy to have her back. She gave any place she was class just by her presence.

"I think we ought to start a campaign to try to get the church to reopen."

"But didn't it close because there wasn't a high enough attendance?"

"Not exactly. That was part of it, but it mostly closed because Pastor Calvin retired, and we couldn't find anyone to take his place. No one who was willing to come up here to preach for the amount of money that we could afford to pay him."

"I see. There are perks to being our pastor that aren't in the written contract."

"Exactly. Even though the pastor committee tried to explain that to potential candidates, we just didn't have enough time to find the right one before we were forced to close the doors. It would have been foolish to try to keep it open over the winter, and then...one thing led to another, and I guess we just never rebounded."

"I see. That happens at times."

"It does. But I'd like to revisit the situation and reopen if we can."

"We should talk to Gertie and get her take on it."

"Talking to Gertie is getting harder and harder. When's the last time you tried to have a conversation with her?" Fran did not want to be rude, and she also did not want to be mean. And she definitely did not want to gossip, but facts were facts, and Gertie, quite frankly, was not going to be much help.

"I suppose you're right. I've spoken with her occasionally, but I don't typically see her out and about over the winter. I have a tendency to hibernate as well."

"Didn't you guys go to the tropics for a while?" Fran asked, knowing very well that they had.

Vera smiled. "It was beautiful there. If you ever get a chance, you should visit."

"I highly doubt I'll ever get a chance, but I'll certainly keep it in mind."

"What about Pat? Have you said anything to her?" Harry and Pat were the retired couple who often were found sitting on their front porch on a summer evening, enjoying the late breezes and their newfound free time. Their children had all left the nest, so they were empty nesters, now newly retired, and Pat would have time to help.

"I have not. I wanted to come to you first. After all, you kind of banded our ladies together and mostly made us a gardening group. I am proposing that we expand our efforts to the gardens of the soul."

"I like that. Maybe that could be the name of our group. Gardens of the Soul."

"I hadn't considered having a name, but I suppose if we have a project, we ought to have a name as well."

"I'll be on board whatever you do." Vera uncrossed her legs and crossed them in the opposite direction. "I'm all about whatever we can do to make Raspberry Ridge a beautiful place. A church would definitely be an asset."

"Maybe I'll ask Sally. She and her husband are new to the area, but… that might be just the thing to do to get her involved."

"She's probably about the same age as Skyler. Did you check with her?"

"I spoke with Homer. He said that wherever his mother went, Skyler would most likely be going too, since he had hired Skyler as a caretaker."

That was news to Vera as her brows went up, and her mouth formed an O. "I wasn't sure whether she would be staying or not."

"It's my understanding that she doesn't have a choice, but that's just town gossip, and I won't repeat it."

But she would say it the first time. Which she just did.

"I'm actually on my way to go see her. I bought a small gift for her, just something to welcome the baby and something to make her feel like Raspberry Ridge might be a good place for her to put down roots. I don't think there's anything going on between her and Homer, although he did not deny that the baby was his. So I could be wrong about that."

"I guess time will tell. That's not really something that I need to know. Although, if Skyler wants to talk about it, it probably would be nice for her to feel like there's a group of ladies who will support her in town. She...must feel awfully lonely being here without any family or friends. At least, none that I know of."

"I don't know of any either. But maybe I can ask her and see if I can get a little bit of information on her past. You're certainly welcome to come along if you want to, I'm headed that way now, as soon as I finish my tea and our visit."

"Maybe I'll wait and visit her later. I probably ought to get a gift myself, that was a really great idea. Thanks for suggesting it."

They chatted a bit more, and then Fran finished her tea, took her leave, and went to visit the newest member of their community.

Sixteen

"That's a beautiful flower." Skyler pointed to a pink flower that bloomed with brilliant profusion amongst the weeds in Gertie's garden. "What kind is it?"

Gertie smiled. "That's an iris. They are some of the first flowers to bloom in the spring after tulips. They're pretty hardy, and I have a lot of them. Their green stays pretty well into the winter."

"I see."

Skyler had noticed that no matter what shape Gertie's mind was in, she always knew the names of her flowers. Whatever Alzheimer's did to her, it wasn't taking that part of her brain away. Although, there were times when they were sitting at the dinner table, or in the evening when they all gathered around in the living room together, when Gertie didn't know who Homer was. It was hard on him.

Sometimes she wondered if God was really good, why didn't He take away the part of her brain that knew the names of flowers and not the part of her brain that knew the name of her child.

She pushed the stroller a little farther into the garden. The back was a little bit straight for Saylor, but she'd been able to adjust it with a blanket and get Saylor tucked in nice and snug so she didn't worry about her falling out.

Saylor seemed to love to be outside and in the garden in particular. She had just turned three weeks old, and Skyler was feeling much more like her old self.

She still only had two rather shaggy outfits to wear, but she was grateful to be decently clothed.

Modestly clothed.

But she hadn't started getting paid yet, and when she did, she owed Homer so much, she wasn't sure she could ever spend any money without feeling guilty about it until she had paid him back. He had said he didn't want payback, but...she still felt like she owed him. A lot of the time, he didn't seem like he even liked her, although she never wondered whether or not he liked Saylor. That was a given.

She kind of thought he would do anything for her. And contrary to what she had been concerned about, Saylor's crying did not bother Homer at all. In fact, in the evening when she had her crying, fussy spell, Homer would actually go over and pick her up and walk with her, pacing back and forth in the living room.

Skyler had been reading some books from the study like he'd suggested. Although she hadn't quite gotten up the nerve to go in and read while he was working.

For some reason, he hadn't seemed to work much for the first two weeks that Saylor was home, but he'd been back to work for the last week or so, and even though she wasn't technically watching his mother, Skyler basically spent her day with her.

Sometimes she even cooked supper. Depending on how difficult Saylor was being and how much pain Skyler was in. She had to admit that was all fading, and things were getting back to normal.

"Good afternoon, ladies," a voice said, causing Skyler to turn around. It wasn't often that they had visitors. Raspberry Ridge was a small, quiet town. The kids must have still been in school, because especially during the day, there was hardly ever anyone else about.

For all Skyler knew, there might not be any kids living in Raspberry Ridge.

"Fran! How nice to see you. Come on into the garden. We were just admiring the irises."

"They're early this year," Fran said as she came in, carrying a small package and closing the gate behind her.

"They are. I was just teaching Skyler what they're called. These ones are my favorite. They seem rather rare."

"Typically you see the purple ones, although my favorite color is red," Fran said, coming closer. She seemed to want to peer down at the baby, so Skyler moved the stroller around, careful to keep Saylor out of the sun but pointing it so that Miss Fran could look in and then coo over the baby.

"Isn't she sweet? And she has your nose. That's really nice. I bet she has your eyes too, but they're closed."

"She's been sleeping a lot during the day. Then she's up at night."

"Then you wake her up during the day so she's ready to sleep at night. Otherwise, you'll never get anything done, and you'll die of exhaustion."

Skyler hadn't considered waking Saylor up. That was a novel idea, and she knew her mouth was hanging open.

"You hadn't thought of that." Fran looked pleased with herself to have given her a bit of advice that could potentially help her.

"I hadn't. But...I don't know if I can bring myself to wake up a sleeping baby or not. When she goes to sleep, it's not that I don't like interacting with her, it's just...a break, you know?"

"And you've only been a mother for three weeks. Wait until it's been longer. You'll consider smacking them over the head with a hammer to get them to go to sleep."

Skyler did not think that would ever happen.

"I'm kidding. Don't look so horrified. I certainly never hit any of my children with a hammer. On the head or anywhere else." She mumbled under her breath, "That's mostly because I didn't know where the hammers were kept in the house, but that's beside the point."

"Well, I do admit that naptime is a nice time, and I'll have to consider what you said. Maybe especially in the evening, although that seems to be her fussy time."

"Many babies have a fussy time in the evening."

Skyler had figured that out, after looking online on the phone that Homer had gotten her.

She couldn't call anyone, although Homer had given her his number. But she didn't have the numbers of any of her friends in Chicago. She might have been able to figure out Kylie's number, but Kylie wasn't going to be answering her phone.

"I brought this for the baby. It's kind of a housewarming gift, but…I heard you were staying." She held up a gift bag, and Skyler took it.

"That's right."

"Skyler and I have so many things to talk about. I just don't think I could let her go even if she wanted to. Where are you from, dear?" Gertie said, and just like that, the clarity that she had was replaced by the fuzzy look in her eye that Skyler often saw, when Gertie had no idea who she was talking to or even sometimes where she was.

But she always knew the names of her flowers.

"Oh, by the way, I wanted to show you this rosebush. Now, it's a little bit of a tricky thing to grow roses this far north, but this rosebush is very hardy. I have to baby it along a bit, but it's the softest color of lavender when it blooms. You just wait." She stopped and looked around at the sky. "I'm not sure what time of year it is, but I don't think it's quite ready to bloom yet."

"It's May, Gertie dear," Fran said, patting Gertie's arm.

"All right. May it is. And who are you?" Gertie said, looking at her with confusion in her eyes like she couldn't figure out why someone she didn't know was touching her.

"I'm your friend Fran, and this is Skyler. Apparently your new best friend."

"Oh no, that's Linda. And have you seen her sweet little baby boy?"

Skyler held her breath while Gertie continued. "My husband just adores that baby. In fact, Linda's been thinking about leaving him here while I take care of him. Wouldn't that be nice?"

Fran didn't say anything, and Skyler wondered if perhaps Fran knew exactly what had gone on all those years before.

After listening to Gertie talk, Skyler thought she had pieced together the mystery. Maybe someday she would know Fran well enough that she could ask her. But she didn't want to seem like a gossip. She also didn't want to disturb Homer's carefully ordered life if he didn't know.

"Aren't you going to open your gift, girl?" Fran asked, pasting a smile on her face that didn't quite reach her eyes.

"Oh. Of course. It was so sweet of you to get me a gift."

"I knew exactly what I needed to get you after seeing you in my store when you first came. You know, you were so heavy with child that day, that I just had to follow you back to the bathroom, because I was afraid you might have been in labor. No one has ever delivered a baby in that bathroom before, and I was hoping that you would not be the first."

Skyler smiled. So her idea of Fran following her back because she was afraid that she was going to steal something was totally unfounded. Maybe that thought made her smile just a little bit bigger than it had been.

"I wasn't in labor then. But my Braxton Hicks started soon... I guess they weren't Braxton Hicks."

"No. They were the real thing, if you delivered a baby before midnight that evening." Her brows puckered. "Who were you looking for when you left in such a hurry? I thought you mumbled something about somebody waiting for you."

Skyler considered. She hadn't thought about whether or not she should tell the world what happened to her. She wanted to talk it over with Homer first, but she just hadn't. Maybe she hadn't been brave enough, or maybe she hadn't figured out whether Homer liked her, or whether he was just putting up with her because of her baby. He seemed infatuated with Saylor.

"My boyfriend dropped me off so I could use the restroom. And then he left."

"He left left?" Fran asked, like there was a different kind of left other than the kind where someone drives off without their girlfriend in the car with them.

"Yeah. That kind of left. Left left."

"And you haven't talked to him since?"

"No. I haven't."

"He didn't even come back to see how you were?"

"No. He didn't."

"Haven't you called him?"

"I left my phone in the car. Along with my purse."

"So he didn't drive off on accident."

"No. I don't think that he forgot that he was going somewhere with his girlfriend and then went back home without her. I'm pretty sure that he knew all along what he was doing. But yeah, he also knows that I didn't have a purse, cards, cash, or even a phone."

"That is sad."

Skyler resisted the urge to hang her head. She felt like there was something wrong with her when her boyfriend wouldn't even hang around or that he would drop her off and leave. It had been a while since she thought about it. Although it had only been three weeks since it happened, but with all the things that were happening with Saylor, and with taking care of Gertie, and feeling better herself, she had managed to put it out of her mind.

Now the feeling stole over her, the feeling of not being good enough, of being so terrible that her own fiancé would abandon her.

"I actually think it worked out for the good," Gertie said, jumping into the conversation like she had understood every word. "I have Skyler here with me, and Homer just absolutely adores Saylor. I think it's just what our family needed. Sometimes God works in mysterious ways, and sometimes He gives you exactly what you need, when you didn't even know you needed it."

Gertie put her arm around Skyler as though she understood that Skyler had been feeling bad.

"Now, are you going to finish unwrapping that gift?"

"Yeah. I am." She smiled, feeling like Gertie's embrace was almost like a mother's hug. Not that she had had many of those; she couldn't even remember her real mother. Didn't know her name or anything about her. Other than she apparently didn't want her since someone on the street had found her in a garbage can.

If anybody ever wondered what happened to those babies that they heard about on the news that were found in trash cans, Skyler was the result of one of those. Of course, after being in foster care for a while, she'd gone to live with her gram, and got to know her aunt, but then she'd gone back into the system after her gram didn't want her anymore.

She finished taking the paper off and gasped with pleasure.

"It's the onesie that says Raspberry Ridge is a great place to grow up!" A cute little onesie that was absolutely the perfect size for Saylor.

"Most babies are between seven and nine pounds. I figured it would fit her now, and then you have to come in and exchange it for a bigger size when she grows a little."

"I can do that?"

"We make exceptions for residents of Raspberry Ridge sometimes." Fran gave her a smile that made Skyler think that Fran didn't mean to make her sad. "Gertie, I was hoping that maybe you and Skyler are still going to participate in the gardening club this year."

"Well, of course. Yes. We wouldn't miss it, would we, Linda?" Gertie said with obvious enjoyment in her voice.

"No, we definitely wouldn't," Skyler said, meeting Fran's eyes as she lifted her brows in question at Gertie's use of the name Linda. She shrugged her shoulders, trying to let Fran know that she just rolled with it. There was no point in getting into a big argument about something that didn't really matter anyway. She could answer to the name Linda.

"Well, I have another special project that I'm hoping to work on, so when we get together, we'll be talking about that too."

"Oh, that's nice. What are you going to do? Expand the garden?" Gertie said.

"No. What we're actually going to do is figure out how we can get the church to reopen. Raspberry Ridge should have a church. After all, you drive through any town east of the Mississippi, and there are churches on every corner practically. Why, I've heard of towns in the northeast that have more churches than restaurants."

"When our church was open, we had more churches than restaurants," Gertie said, and Skyler thought that was pretty reasonable coming from someone who was sometimes in and out of reality.

"That's a good point. You know what, this town could use a restaurant too. But someone else is going to have to spearhead that since I have all I can do to keep a souvenir shop open and be in the garden club and now I have this new project. I'm excited to have your help."

"We're excited to help you, aren't we, Gertie?" Skyler said, thinking that it might be really nice to have a church in town. She wanted her daughter to grow up in church. She wanted a lot for her daughter. Love, acceptance, and faith in a higher power. No. Faith in God. That's what she wanted.

Seventeen

Homer sat on the recliner, Saylor snuggled in his arm. She hadn't quite gotten to her fussy stage this evening, but he was prepared when she did. He didn't mind walking the floor with her and in fact found it easier for himself to think. He wasn't used to taking evenings off, and he typically worked as long as he wanted to, often not stopping until eleven o'clock or even midnight.

But now, he found that he actually got more done when he took a break with...his family.

Could he consider Skyler and Saylor and his mom all sitting at the table his family? It felt like family.

Anyway, he ate with them, spent some time in the evening with them. Sometimes they chatted, but for the most part, Skyler was rather quiet and Homer could think about the problems he faced in his job. Working on them, moving them around in his mind, figuring them out, and then, once everyone else went to bed, he could go upstairs and work on them some more.

He got almost twice as much done since they started this new routine. He had Skyler to thank.

Of course, taking two weeks off work had been helpful as well. He hadn't had a vacation in a really long time.

His mother's soft snores were the only things that broke the stillness of the evening.

The days were getting longer and longer, and daylight had not quite faded.

He wanted to walk Skyler and Saylor down to the beach. They had to go around the bluffs, and the hike was not exactly arduous but a little bit more than he thought Skyler could handle.

She wasn't walking quite as gingerly as she had been, and she seemed like she had more energy.

"Payment for last week will deposit in your account on Friday morning. It should be there when you wake up."

He spoke into the stillness of the room, his mother's gentle snort the only sign that the sound of his voice might have interrupted her nap.

Skyler's head jerked up. She looked around, then looked back at him. "Me?"

She was so cute. His mother had taken to her. Almost more than she had taken to him. It was a little bit disconcerting. It might have been more so, if his mother hadn't insisted on calling Skyler Linda ninety percent of the time.

At least she didn't know Skyler's name any more than she knew his. But Skyler had a gentle way about her that kept his mother in hand. Sometimes he and his mother had gone rounds about what she was allowed to do and what she wasn't, and Skyler didn't fight with her. But somehow, she just guided her into doing what Skyler wanted her to do.

Homer had watched her several times, shaking his head each time. He couldn't quite figure out what Skyler was doing that he wasn't and how she was able to get the results that she did, and he couldn't.

"Yeah. I'm not expecting you to spend all day every day with my mother and not get paid."

"Oh." Skyler allowed her book to fall to her lap as she seemed to look to the ceiling for guidance. "I already owe you so much. Honestly, I haven't been doing much with your mother at all. Just... We enjoy spending time together. Even if she does call me Linda."

"I noticed that. Do you have any idea why?"

From the look on her face as she quickly looked toward her lap, Homer would say she did.

"Is there something you want to tell me?"

"I don't know. It's all conjecture. And you know that your mom sometimes isn't quite…"

"You don't have to tell me. I certainly know. But tell me what it is that you're thinking. Why she thinks you're Linda."

"Well, obviously Linda was one of her friends."

"I knew that. They had Bible study together. She and Linda were close before I was born apparently. Really close. I…heard her talk about Linda a good bit as I was growing up, but then it kind of faded away, and I didn't hear too much about her. I don't know what happened to her."

"Yeah. I… I have the feeling that Linda had a baby boy."

"I see."

"The reason I think that is when she calls me Linda, she keeps insisting that Saylor is actually a boy. Even though she's watched me change her diaper, and she sees me dressing her in pink. Sometimes she scolds me for it. I've quit arguing with her, but she's worried that…I'm going to do damage to Saylor because I dress her in pink. Because boys shouldn't wear pink. According to your mom."

"I'm kind of glad she feels that way. I'm not overly fond of the color myself, but that doesn't really answer any questions I have though."

Skyler was quiet for a bit, and she chewed on her lip. An obvious sign that she was thinking.

He let her think and allowed his mind to wander a little. She cooked supper every night for the last week. And he hadn't asked. He just got out of his room to go down and make it, and it was already made. Or she talked in the morning about what she was going to make.

He had actually said that he would run to the grocery store if she needed him to, and she'd taken him up on that several times. It was the least he could do if she was going to cook.

That was the main reason he had gotten her bank account information and decided to pay her immediately. It was a little more complicated than what he had expected to have one employee on payroll, but it was a necessary evil. He was going to have to do it for someone. It might as well be Skyler.

He knew he was fooling himself. The more time he spent with Skyler, the less he wanted her to leave him.

"Do you think it's possible that...that Linda was your mother?"

He had been so deep in thought that her question didn't register at first.

When he heard it, he must have moved so much that he woke Saylor, and she started to whimper.

Immediately he started to gently rock her. Normally he didn't mind getting up and pacing the floor with her, but...that idea was radical.

He wanted to say no. In fact, no had come to his lips immediately, but he knew that Skyler wasn't saying anything to hurt him. In fact, she went out of her way to make things easier for him. Taking care of his mother, making lunch and supper, and heating leftovers for breakfast. She made sure the dishes were taken care of, and she knew what his favorite drink was, when he was expecting coffee, and how he took it. She had paid attention, and sometimes he didn't even notice because she just did it so smoothly.

"I want to say no." He paused. "But I suppose I'm unable to answer that question."

"Obviously you're a man, so it's not surprising to me that I don't really see anything of your mother on your face. I...kinda studied it. I hope that doesn't sound weird, but as my suspicion has grown, I tried to figure out if this could be wrong. Your mom offered, and I took her up on it, to show me childhood pictures. Even then, she's so fair, with almond-shaped eyes, and your eyes are just different, your skin darker, your hair darker too, she just...doesn't really look anything like you."

"Or I don't look anything like her." He didn't need to correct her. It just came out.

She nodded and didn't seem to mind that he had corrected her.

He knew she was a little sensitive about that from the ride home from the hospital. He didn't know what to do about it. He couldn't change the way he was, and he didn't want to change the way she was. Even though she might not believe it. Although he never told her.

There were a lot of things that he'd never told her. Things that sometimes wanted to come out of his mouth and he had to hold back.

"I guess I'll have to think about that. It's a total shift from what I believed all of my life. And while I want to emphatically deny it, I am not sure you might not be onto something."

It might just be the ramblings of his mother in the throes of Alzheimer's.

"That's not really everything."

"It's not?"

"No. I... She talks a lot about Phil. Who is Phil?"

"Phil is my father."

Eighteen

Skyler sat there stunned. She had concluded, almost decisively, that Phil was the father of Linda's baby. She thought that baby was Homer, and she thought that perhaps Gertie had somehow ended up raising it.

"What's that look for?" Homer asked, although the tone of his voice declared he thought he might not want to know.

"I wasn't sure who Phil was, and just from hearing your mom talk…" She glanced over at the chair where his mother still snored softly. She didn't know what kind of state of mind she would be in when she woke up, but she didn't want to talk about this and upset either Gertie or Homer. It wasn't her job to try to spin the family dynamics into chaos.

"Just from hearing your mom talk, I kind of pieced together an idea of what I thought might have happened. Linda had a baby, and Gertie raised the baby. I'm not sure what happened to Linda, but I'm pretty sure the father of her baby was Phil."

Homer looked stunned. She almost offered to take Saylor from him, but she didn't want to insult him. He was so careful with the baby. She knew he wouldn't do anything to harm her.

"Wow. I... I never thought anything of the sort. I just...assumed he was my dad and Mom was my mom..."

"Yeah. And I could be totally off base. I think I'm piecing things together, but you know how your mom can be. She...isn't always totally coherent."

"No. I know. I also know that you're not doing anything on purpose to hurt anyone. I'm the one who asked. And I guess maybe I uncovered more than I wanted to know."

"Yeah. I wasn't going to say anything to you until I knew for sure. But what am I supposed to do? Go to Fran? Would she know?"

"Actually, Fran probably would know. She was part of the Bible study for a while with Mom and Linda and Karen. I think Karen was in on it too."

"Does Karen still live in town?"

"Yeah. She and Mom had a falling out a while ago, and I'm not sure what it was over. It was...about the time my dad left, I guess. So, ten, fifteen years ago."

"All right. I'm not sure if what I figured out makes any sense at all, but I guess I could ask."

"Karen would know."

"Would you mind if I asked?" she asked, feeling like she was pushing things a little bit. She didn't want him to feel like he had to say yes to her.

He shrugged a shoulder. "If people know, they know."

"I guess I could ask in a way that doesn't give away what I'm thinking. Maybe in a roundabout way, without implicating anybody in anything."

"Don't worry too much about it. We survived small-town gossip before, and I'm sure we'll continue to weather the storms. But honestly, for the most part, Raspberry Ridge is a great place. Even though Karen and Mom don't talk, they're not unkind to each other. They would still nod at each other if they passed on the sidewalk or met on the beach. They just don't do Bible study together anymore."

"That's sad."

"Yeah. People have a tendency to throw friendships away like they don't mean anything. But a good friend is really hard to find. And from what I understand from what Mom has said, the Bible study that she did with those ladies was life-changing for her, and for them too, I think."

"The Bible has a tendency to be life-changing to people."

"Yeah. You're absolutely right about that. It might be the Bible, rather than the friends."

"The friendships are important. And...you form bonds that can't ever be broken." She supposed she was thinking about Kylie and how she still felt like Kylie maybe was looking over her shoulder at times, no matter how whimsical that might be.

She wished Kylie would have been able to come to Raspberry Ridge with her, to get out of the drugs and alcohol and the bondage they represented, and to be set free. Free to have a life that wasn't controlled by substance abuse.

Maybe that was just a part of her fairy-tale thinking, and Kylie wouldn't have been happy in a small town.

But she kind of thought she would.

"Sorry about your friend."

"It's okay. She... She was my one good friend. I would have trusted her with anything."

As soon as she said that, she remembered the money that Kylie had stolen from her. It was funny. In her mind, she built Kylie up to some kind of almost superhuman thing, and she conveniently forgot that Kylie hadn't always been a good friend. Although Kylie hadn't meant anything by the theft. She was just feeding the habit that she couldn't shake.

Saylor started to fuss, and Homer put his recliner down. "Sounds to me like it's about time for a walk this evening. Too bad Mom isn't up. I think it's warm enough we could walk outside."

"She loves being outside. She hardly ever cries out there."

She wished that they could take a stroll. Not that it would be like a family, although maybe that was part of it. But just... It would be nice to take a stroll on the sidewalk with a handsome man, one who treated her well and was kind to her daughter.

She wanted to ask why he never got married. From the way he was treating her and her daughter, he would make some woman an excellent husband.

But there were definitely things that were none of her business, and that was probably one of them.

Nineteen

It had been four weeks since she had Saylor, and Skyler felt pretty good as she carefully opened the door to Homer's study and walked in.

This was the first time she'd taken him up on his offer for her to read in his study while he worked. It just seemed...a little bit intrusive.

But she enjoyed being near him, even when they weren't talking. Sometimes in the evening, they sat for an hour or more without saying anything while his mother softly snored in the background, and Saylor slept or, as was more likely now, maybe cooed a little. Or even smiled.

At least Skyler swore that she smiled, although Homer said that he had looked it up and babies didn't smile until they were six weeks old.

Sometimes he was pretty confident about what he knew. And rightly so. She knew he was very intelligent, but sometimes intelligence didn't translate into common sense.

Not that her common sense and street smarts got her very far.

Except...maybe it had. Or maybe that was the Lord just opening up doors she wasn't expecting.

Regardless, she held the book that she had been reading tight to her chest as she knocked softly before she continued to pull the door open.

Homer looked over his shoulder, since his desk faced out the window, gave her a little smile, and then with narrowed eyes turned back to his computer.

It looked like the entire screen was filled with numbers or letters or something. She couldn't quite see from where she stood, other than it was very, very full.

She had no idea what he was doing. He didn't often talk about his work, but she knew that it was complicated.

Knowing that and also knowing how much he had done for her when she had first come, she had been doing everything she could to take all the burden of the home off his shoulders.

Now he only interacted with his mother when he wanted to, and she cooked every meal and washed his clothes as well. She had caught him one day taking his basket downstairs and told him that she would switch them from the washer to the dryer; she had done that, plus folded them, put them back in the basket, and carried them back upstairs.

He had given her a little bit of a hassle about carrying the basket, but she pointed out that she carried her basket and his mother's baskets, and she might as well carry his basket as well.

He closed his mouth into a tight line, like he didn't realize that she had been doing so much.

But that was after Saylor was two and a half weeks old, and she was mostly recovered. At that time, she told him that if he wanted her to wash his clothes, she would, he could just let her know.

He shrugged and said that she could go in his room and get them anytime she wanted to.

So, she'd taken to washing them twice a week.

It seemed like someone with his lifestyle probably had enough clothes to last the entire week, but she did not.

She left the door open just a crack so she could hear the baby if she started to cry and also hear his mother's footsteps if she got up as well.

They had locks on all the doors, so she knew his mother wouldn't be leaving them, but sometimes she got in the kitchen and started making something, then forgot what she was making halfway through, leaving the burners on or the refrigerator door hanging wide open or something like that.

Skyler didn't particularly mind, but she also didn't want the house to burn down around them.

So she left the door cracked and walked softly over to one of the comfortable-looking recliners.

There was a blanket lying over it, and she smiled. It was bigger than the blanket that Homer had bought for Saylor but made of similar material, so soft and cuddly, and perfect for wrapping oneself up and sitting in a chair and reading for a little bit.

She was reading a book about how important it was to read the Bible. Maybe that was irony, but it had made her decide that maybe she should start reading the Bible through. She wanted to ask Homer if he ever had. She bit her lip. Maybe he would want to talk to her about it a little. She would enjoy discussing it with him.

Regardless, she had been sitting in the chair reading so long that she had gotten wrapped up in the book, when Homer's voice startled her.

"I have that part finished, and I was going to take a little break. Just a stand up and walk around the room break."

"Oh. So you can talk to me."

He nodded, smiling a little that she had figured out what he was saying. "Everything going okay today?"

"It is. I hope you...don't mind that I'm here. I know you said it was okay—"

"And I meant that. You're welcome here anytime. I liked knowing that you were behind me."

"It's very cozy in here, and I love this blanket."

"I picked it up at the store. I saw it and thought of you." He didn't say anything more, but his eyes bore into hers, and she couldn't tear her gaze away.

She wasn't sure exactly what he was saying, but...the idea that he thought of her when he saw the blanket, and bought the blanket, and then put it in here, inviting her into his study... Maybe she was reading too much into it, but her stomach started churning, low and slow.

"You're so considerate," she finally whispered.

"I wouldn't consider myself considerate. You... You make me that way."

"No. I don't get any credit for the person that you are. It's all you."

He shook his head, as though brushing her words away, and then he said, "I did a little digging on what you said."

"About Linda and Phil?"

He nodded. "I think you might be right. I don't know if you asked anyone, but I saw a picture of Linda. She has eyes that are shaped exactly the way mine are. And I have her dark hair. It's even curly."

"That doesn't mean anything." Skyler meant her words as reassurance.

Homer lifted his shoulder. "Maybe. Maybe not."

"I haven't gotten out to talk to Karen. It's been raining for the past week. We need the rain for the flowers, or so your mom says, but Saylor shouldn't be out in it. And I can hardly go anywhere without her."

"For four weeks, you haven't gone anywhere without her."

"I don't mind." She wasn't sure what he was saying, but she wanted to be quick to reassure him. She wasn't complaining.

"I asked Vera if she would come watch my mom today. She offered to watch the baby as well, so that would be up to you, but... I wanted to know if you wanted to take a walk?"

She was speechless for a moment. He just asked her to walk with him. And he'd already gotten the sitter lined up. Maybe he thought she was inside too much. Maybe he thought she was working too hard. But he didn't say that.

Of course, he didn't say that he wanted to walk because he wanted to be with her either. That would have meant something.

"All right. That sounds like fun."

"We can plan on it after supper. I...wanted to talk to you a little bit."

"Uh, okay," she said, realizing that he had just made it so they would have some private time. Which was fine. Although she couldn't imagine what he wanted to talk about. Unless something she was doing wasn't satisfactory. But he could talk about that with her now, right? He didn't really need to hire someone to watch his mom and take her away from the house.

Or maybe he was going to send his mom to an adult day care, and she was going to be out of a job.

Don't borrow trouble.

He strode around the room, and almost casually came over and stopped beside her chair.

"You've made a lot of changes in this house and made it feel more like a home. I hadn't realized how I'd allowed things to decline with Mom slipping away. You brought that all back."

"All I'm doing is cooking and washing clothes and doing a little bit of housework."

"No. You bring smiles and happiness. I look forward to supper. And you let me hold Saylor. I definitely am grateful for that. I don't think I've mentioned it, but I work a lot better after I spend a little time downstairs with you and Saylor and my mom too of course."

"That makes sense. To get your mind off your work and allow it to kind of hum along in the background while your consciousness focuses on something else."

He nodded, and they spent a few moments in silence, each lost in thought.

She held up her book. "Have you ever read the Bible through? This book is telling me how important it is to know what it says."

"I have. Multiple times. Used to be I'd read it through every year, but I kinda let that habit fall by the wayside. It's probably a good one to pick back up."

"I never have, but I want to."

"You want to do it together?" he asked, and his words were low and sent a shiver down her backbone. Who would have thought talking about reading the Bible together could be romantic?

But it felt that way.

"I'd really love to."

"You mind getting up early in the morning? We could do it at sunrise."

Sunrise was one of her favorite times of the day, although with Saylor, she wasn't always up at that time.

"I'd love to." And that was the honest truth. She'd go without sleep to have not just the Bible, but the Bible and Homer together.

"All right then. Do you want to start tomorrow?"

"Yes."

"Do you have a Bible?"

Her eyes opened wide. "Actually... I don't."

"While there are plenty of apps that you could get and read on your phone, how about we hold off a week and order actual Bibles? Two of the same. That way we could read together, out of the exact same Bible."

"I'd love that. But you have to let me pay for mine."

"No. It was my idea. You could get a used copy for a dollar, or I can order brand-new copies and pay a little more. You shouldn't have to pay more just because I want something extra."

She closed her mouth, but she really wanted to argue. He had been kinder to her than she deserved, and she didn't like the feeling of being in his debt, although he never made her feel like she owed him anything. In fact, on the contrary, he made her feel like he was just being kind. She was the one who felt guilty about it.

"All right. I probably ought to get back to work." He put his hand on her shoulder, a casual touch that almost felt like more. Her shoulder heated, and she wanted to bend her arm so that her fingers brushed over his.

She tried to keep herself from doing it, but her arm started to move, just as his fingers left her shoulder, trailing down just a little, or maybe it was her imagination. She wasn't sure.

They didn't say anything else, and he went over and sat back down in his chair, waking his screen up and starting into work.

It wasn't long after that that the baby cried, and she got up to go get her, wondering what the evening would bring.

Twenty

Homer stood at the sink, rinsing off the dishes before he put them in the dishwasher. Supper had been delicious, and Skyler had asked him to go pick up a few more groceries sometime this week.

He thought about asking her to go with him this evening, but he had been looking forward to walking to the bluffs with her. Maybe holding her hand. He...wasn't entirely sure exactly what he wanted, other than to spend some time with her. Time alone.

As alone as they could be if they were walking the public streets of Raspberry Ridge.

He was a little disappointed she hadn't dressed up more. Not that he typically noticed what she wore, but usually it was baggy, a nondescript shirt with nondescript pants.

He was pretty sure she could fit back into her regular clothes and kind of wondered why she wasn't wearing them.

And then, it hit him. She didn't have any clothes.

How could he have been so dumb? It was going on four weeks that she had been in his home, and he hadn't even noticed that she was wearing the same outfit over and over again? But looking back, he could tell that it had been. Maybe two outfits. Something that she had been given at the hospital, he was pretty sure, and the outfit that she had been wearing when she came. Pants for pregnant women. He knew they were called something, but he couldn't remember what. Maternity pants? And a large, flowing shirt.

Well, he would try to rectify that, but he wasn't sure how. Should he just buy clothes for her? Or should he ask her to order them and he would pay for them? No. That was definitely out. She would not allow him to pay for them. And if he asked her to order clothes, she would feel like he was criticizing what she was wearing, like it wasn't good enough or something.

Girls liked clothes. Surely. Of course, he didn't really know much about girls, having not spent much time around them.

Skyler was different though. He felt comfortable with her. Comfortable in a way he never had with anyone else. Maybe it was the way she was always looking for a way to serve him. Always looking to see what she could do to make his life easier. Always taking on more so he could do less.

But he didn't want her to do everything and him do nothing, which is why he was standing at the sink, rinsing off dishes.

"Hello! Anyone home?" Vera's voice rang out as she knocked on the door, probably in the process of opening it. That's the way most of the neighbors were around Raspberry Ridge. They didn't particularly stand on formality where they waited until someone opened the door before they came in.

"We're in the kitchen. We just finished up supper. Perfect timing," he called.

"Vera? I didn't know you were coming today," his mother said, and Homer said a silent prayer of thanks that she was in her right mind. At least for a little bit. It would make it easier for Vera if she wasn't belligerent. She had been getting more and more like that, particularly in the evening. Probably because she was tired from a long day.

Skyler seemed to have a way with her, but Homer, more often than not, ended up arguing with her.

"Oh my goodness, it smells delicious in here. I think I should have arrived earlier," she said, coming in, a whiff of something classy and bright trailing behind her.

He should get Skyler perfume. Maybe not quite like that, something a little younger. Something that made him think of wildflowers and lake breezes and big, happy smiles.

He shook his head. He was thinking way too much about Skyler, and he needed to stop. Although, he really was going to buy her clothes. Maybe Vera would know what size she was.

"Can I talk to you for a minute?" he asked as he put the last dish in the dishwasher and closed it, hitting the buttons to start it before he straightened and looked at Vera.

"Sure," she said.

He glanced over at Skyler who was sitting in the corner, nursing her baby under a blanket. "We'll be right back," Homer said, lifting his brows at Skyler.

She nodded. "I should be done here soon, and then Saylor should be good for the evening."

"Oh my goodness, I didn't even see you over there in the corner. You're feeding the baby. That's perfect timing."

"I tried to time it so it would be easiest for you."

"I appreciate that." Vera smiled, and then she followed Homer out of the kitchen.

He took her across the hall into the formal living room where he closed the door.

"What's going on? You look a little serious," Vera said, smiling gently, as though to ease whatever burden Homer was carrying and make the conversation easier.

Homer figured he might as well just jump into it. He didn't know how to open a conversation like this. It wasn't exactly something he'd ever talked to anyone about before.

He'd never even bought his mother clothes.

"I know I'm probably the last person to know, but I figured out just a few minutes ago that Skyler has been wearing the same clothes since she came home from the hospital. I know she's making enough money to buy clothes for herself, but I wanted to buy some for her, and I know if I ask her to pick them out, she'll feel like she needs to pay for them. Plus, she might feel like I'm criticizing her outfits, and I'm not."

"It's fine. You don't have to explain to me. You want to do something nice for the girl that's living under your roof. And if someone needs clothes, it's a little awkward because we don't typically see that nowadays, but it's totally fine." Vera smiled gently, and he immediately felt better.

But he was crossing way too many lines and didn't want to think about it.

"I need to know her size. I can't ask her, or she'll know what I'm doing and protest."

"I understand. I think it's very sweet." Vera closed her mouth and thought for a little bit, squinting her eyes. She sighed deeply. "My background is in design, and I'm supposed to notice the details. I would say that Skyler is very close to my size. Slightly shorter though." She named a size, and Homer immediately took out his phone.

"One second. I better write this down. I don't want to forget and, after going through all this trouble, end up buying the wrong size anyway."

"Well, you can always call me and ask if you forget, I don't have problems picturing things in my mind, and even if I don't remember what size I told you, I can figure it out again."

"All right. That's reassuring, but I'd rather not have to do that. I'm going to order them tonight after we get back."

"I got the idea that this might be a...date?" Vera said the word delicately and carefully, like she didn't want to cross any boundaries or ask something that wasn't her business.

"I don't know what it is. I just... She hasn't been away from the baby since she was born, and she's been watching my mother for almost as long. I just wanted her to be able to get out of the house. And I guess... I wanted to go with her." Maybe that did make it a date. But since they lived together, he wasn't sure what that made them. Employer and employee, but...he didn't want to think about it that way. She was more to him than that. But he didn't really want to look at how much more she was.

"Fair enough." Vera smiled, and it wasn't the smile of someone who was upset that they didn't get the information that they wanted, but it was a real, friendly, happy smile.

"Thanks for doing this."

"I'll come and chat with your mother anytime. It gets me out of my house, and if nothing else, we can take a walk in the flower garden and talk plants. Maybe we'll even be able to get our hands dirty."

It was hard for him to picture Miss Vera getting her hands dirty, but if she insisted.

He opened the door, and she led the way back across the hall to the kitchen where Skyler was done feeding the baby and had her over her shoulder, patting her back gently. Just as they walked in, Saylor let out a big burp.

"Oh goodness. She has good timing," Skyler said, laughing a little and looking embarrassed.

"That's what babies are supposed to do," Vera said sweetly. "And I'm glad you got all that, so now I just get the happy, full, content baby."

"You can leave the baby here with us, Linda. We'll take good care of him."

"All right, Gertie. Thank you," Skyler said, and she handed Saylor to Vera with a look. Vera returned it. And Homer didn't miss the exchange. They were smiling, but there was a sadness in both of their eyes.

He understood that. It was kind of how he felt. He loved his mom and appreciated her, and it was hard to watch her slip away.

Skyler gave a few instructions, and he mentioned a few things for Miss Vera to watch out for with his mom, and then, almost before he knew it, he and Skyler had stepped out of the house and walked down the steps to the sidewalk.

It was old and a little cracked in spots, but it wasn't dangerous to walk on, and he pointed toward the bluffs.

"Want to walk that way? I kind of wanted to show you the lake and the view from the bluffs. It's...pretty. Especially as the sun goes down."

"I'd love it. I've been curious about the healing garden, but with the rain this past week, we haven't made it over there."

"I'd love to show that to you too. I haven't been there much myself. But Vera is an award-winning and nationally renowned garden planner, and her husband is a landscaper. They designed it for their son, in memory of him."

"To help with their grief since they lost their child."

Homer nodded but didn't say much. He didn't really know. But the idea of losing Saylor, of her being gone forever, made him sad. To think of her empty crib, her little blanket, not having her to entertain him in the evenings or to fuss and give him a reason to walk.

They walked down the street, which was deserted, unsurprisingly. Sometimes in the summer, tourists would come and park along the bluffs. Sometimes teenagers would sneak there after midnight and use it as a rendezvous. It was a beautiful place. He might have parked there when he had been a teenager, if he had any idea of how to get a girl to do it with him.

He was glad now that he hadn't, but it wasn't necessarily for lack of wanting to. It was more for lack of the company.

Which made him all the more nervous about what he was doing now. He wasn't exactly good at this, and he wasn't sure exactly what *this* was.

"Thank you for inviting me. I haven't been out for a long time, and while I haven't really minded, the thought of getting out today just made my whole afternoon happier. I don't know how to explain it." She lifted her shoulder and also lifted her face to the lake breeze, closing her eyes as it pushed her hair back away from her face and breathing in deeply.

She was so pretty. So...different from him. She laughed easier, smiled a lot more, was more patient with his mother, and was always looking for ways to help others. He wasn't like that at all. He always had some kind of issue or problem he was solving in his head. Working around it, trying to figure things out.

They continued to walk, and he tried to think of something to say to break the silence. Not that it wasn't a comfortable silence, he just wanted to talk with her, now that he had her alone.

"Did you have something you wanted to talk to me about?" Skyler finally said, after they were almost to the garden.

"Uh, I guess I did." He couldn't remember what it was right then though. He just wanted to tell her how pretty she was, how much he wanted to hold her hand, how much he...wanted her to stay. And...be with him? He wasn't sure. But he thought that's where he wanted to go.

"This is the garden." He stopped at the wrought iron gate, a small fence enclosing the entire area. It was black and should have looked somber and austere, but the riotous blooming flowers inside kept anyone from having that impression at all.

"Are we allowed in?" she asked as he put his hand on the latch.

"Yeah. They made it for the residents of Raspberry Ridge, or anyone really. It's a beautiful place to relax. And I can hear the waterfall."

"Oh. I can too. I didn't realize..." She stepped in, and it was like entering an enchanted world. However Vera had designed it, she had flowers blooming almost yearlong, and while the waterfall didn't run in the winter, when there was any chance of it freezing, it ran continuously spring, summer, and fall. The running water made a soothing sound and made the garden a beautiful place of contemplation.

"They have a little stone here for their son." He pointed out the marker that had their son's name on it, his date of birth, and a small, meaningful statement. *Beloved by both father and mother. Sorely missed. Looking forward to our reunion in heaven.*

"Is he buried here?" Skyler asked, wide eyes turning to his.

"No. He's buried in the cemetery not far from town. There's a small one, behind the church. It's...just outside of town and up on a little rise."

"Sounds pretty."

"It is. Not as pretty as this, but a peaceful place."

He reached for her hand, taking it before he said, "Come on. Let me show you the bench. There are several, but I have a favorite."

She allowed her hand to stay in his as he led her away. Maybe he was cheating a little, because he kind of took her hand under the guise of leading her to the bench, but he didn't intend to let go.

In the garden, they'd be safe from the prying eyes of the town. He could...hold her hand, sit close to her, put his arm around her.

Man, he was so terrible at this. He didn't even know what he should do. Didn't know how to...let her know that he wanted to be more than what they were.

Was it fair to her? Probably not if he didn't know what exactly he wanted to be and how devoted he wanted to be. If he didn't have the right intentions, he probably shouldn't be leading her on.

"It's this one," he said, leading her to a bench that was backed by tall grasses, which had not quite grown to their full height yet, where the fountain was a soothing murmur, and the bench faced the bluffs and the lake beyond. It was the best view in the garden and his favorite place to sit. Not that he came here much, especially since he hadn't been able to leave his mom for over a year.

"I can't believe it's been more than twelve months since I've been able to leave my mom. I don't think I came here at all last year."

"Time flies sometimes. We don't pay attention."

"You want to sit for a bit?" he asked.

"If that's okay. It looks like a really relaxing place."

"It is. And...I'd love to sit here with you." There. He said that.

She didn't say anything, other than giving him a small smile, before she sat down.

He allowed her hand to slip out of his as he sat down and, in one motion, put his hand behind her.

"Is this okay?" he asked, looking down into her eyes.

She had them focused on her lap and her hands which she had tightly clenched together. "Yeah. I... I like it."

That was all he needed to hear. It warmed his heart and made it smile. That smile slipped onto his face and curved his mouth.

"I... I don't know what I feel for you, but I think it's more than friends. More than employer. More than I found a girl in my garage, and...I just wanted you to know."

She swallowed and spoke in a small voice. "Thanks. I'm not very good at this. The last man I was with ditched me and never came back for me. It's the kind of thing that marks a girl. You know?" She looked up into his eyes.

"I can promise you I'll never do that."

"I can hear Jeff saying that too. He would promise me anything and then deliver nothing. I..." She lifted her chin. "I was determined to stay with him. I didn't want to be the kind of girl who runs from guy to guy to guy trying to find the perfect guy and never finding him. Because of course he doesn't exist. I thought the issues that I saw in Jeff were just issues that I had to work through. But looking back, I made a bunch of stupid decisions, not the least of which was deciding to be with him."

He sat beside her silently. One part of him was enjoying the closeness, the feeling of having her close. Wanting her closer. The other part of him was discouraged. How was he going to convince her that he was different from Jeff? He had never met the man, but couldn't she see that they weren't the same kind of person?

"I think I might have mentioned that my dad left when I was eighteen?" he asked. That was the only thing he could think of. To tell her his story to get her to understand.

"Yeah. I'm sorry." She didn't say anything more, and he thought about the things that she had heard and that his mom had told her. He pushed all of that aside for now. He couldn't think about that because it would make him crazy. He needed hard facts. Not conjecture.

"You don't have to be sorry. I...loved him, of course. But I guess from about the time I was twelve or so, I suspected that there was something off. I don't know whether there was or not, but it wasn't exactly a surprise when he had some young woman in the car with him, her hair blowing everywhere, his arm around her. I'll never forget that. He had a convertible, and the top was down. She looked so happy, cuddled up beside my dad. Where my mom was supposed to be. And she waved at me as they drove down the street."

He shook his head, remembering.

"I never got that. Why would she wave to me? I was his son. I had a mom and dad, and she had come in between the two of them and split that apart, blew up my world, and yet she was laughing and waved at me, like it was just some big game."

"Sometimes people have a hard time thinking about others when they make decisions."

"I think most people have a hard time. I know she wasn't thinking about anyone but herself and how...happy she was." He said "happy" like it was a bad word. Or like he was talking about garbage instead of a good feeling.

"It probably made you want to grab a hold of her and shake her."

"To say the least." He wanted to do far more than that. He tried not to let himself think nasty, terrible thoughts like that, but it was how he felt.

"Anyway, that's part of the reason I went to Ann Arbor for college. I went to community college even closer, for the first two years, and then transferred, and commuted when I could. I wanted to be home with my mom. I felt like my dad didn't treat her the way she deserved to be treated. She had...taken care of him. I never heard her say an unkind word about him—even after he left with that woman, my mom didn't rip him up one side and down the other. She was...a lady, all the way through."

"I really admire her," Skyler said softly.

"Yeah. Even though she's not always with us anymore, she's still a lady to her toes. She is kind and generous and sweet and loving, and my dad just... He was a jerk. Even when I was growing up, he was never thoughtful of his family. I wanted his approval and attention more than anything, and typically nothing I did was good enough. He had a hard time leaving the hospital, and what I suspect were his girlfriends, to spend time with us. In fact, I suppose it was about the time I turned twelve that he started staying in Chicago for weeks at a time. He had driven home every day before that. I know it's a long drive, but I don't know. I guess he made me feel his family was never that important."

She didn't say anything, like she could have mentioned that he might not even have been his mother's son, and yet she loved him more than his biological father did. He hadn't even thought about that. And didn't know how to fit that in the lens through which he saw his life.

"I know there are other things. Things maybe I don't understand, but what I was trying to say was, he left. And I hated that. And I determined in my heart that I wasn't going to be the kind of man who left. I stayed with my mom. And...I would never be like Jeff."

There, they were just words. Anybody could say them. Jeff could come here tonight and say that he would never leave her again, and it was just a matter of whether or not she saw the character of the man beneath the words.

"I believe you mean it," she said softly, and he wanted to tighten his arm around her, put his hand from the back of the bench onto her shoulder, spreading his fingers through her hair, bring her closer to him. Touch her forehead with his lips.

But it was the first time he had taken her walking, and he just held her hand. He didn't want to move too quickly. Because he heard what she was saying. That she had just been through a really difficult, devastating situation, and she needed some time to recover.

"I guess I didn't say, but I admire you for what you've done. Staying with your mom, taking care of her, working from home, and maybe giving up a more prestigious job."

"Well, that, maybe you haven't noticed, but dealing with people is not exactly my forte, and working from home is actually more of a dream job for me than anything else. I can't take credit for that. But staying with Mom, that's true. I didn't really date in college, mostly because I'm socially awkward, but also I never put the time into trying to figure out how to even ask a girl out, because I didn't have time to do that. Not if I was going to drive home and be with Mom. Of course, I had studying to do as well. And I just realized how ridiculously pathetic that sounds."

"Driving home to be with your mom? No. That's not pathetic. Although, I can see how the world has everything all twisted up. Maybe that's something that they see as being weird. But spoken as someone who didn't have a mom, I would have loved to have had a mom to drive home to. To spend time with. To be the one that she looked for, so she was not alone."

"I'm glad you understand. I just could hardly see her rattling around this old house. It's so big for one person, and she deserves so much better."

"I wish I could say maybe she'd get it, but I guess at this point in her life, that's all there was, and the little she has left. I think it's been a good life."

"I guess you're right. But it's kinda sad to think that she'll never have that person who sees her for who she really is and loves her." He paused for a moment, and then he said softly, "But God does. I hope she realized that. That God loved her exactly the way she was and appreciated the special person she is."

Neither one of them said anything for a while, as though they were digesting that, and then Skyler said softly, "That's what we all want. We look for the person who's going to love us, despite our faults and our flaws, and fill that aching hole inside of us, but maybe that hole is there because God isn't filling us the way we were supposed to let Him. Maybe He created us with a spot that's for Him, and Him only, and we go around trying to fill it with everything else. Money, power, prestige, even love. Romantic love. Rather than God and God's love."

"You've been reading my mom's books, haven't you?"

They laughed a little together, and she nodded her head, her hair brushing his arm, and he resisted the temptation to move his hand so it was touching it.

"I have. And while that wasn't exactly something any of them said, it's definitely something that I can see different things pointing to. I mean, God says, 'thou shalt have no other gods before me,' and He wants us to give Him first place in our lives. Doesn't it make sense that He would have created us to need Him? And we know this, on a fundamental level, but we don't admit it. And then when we feel the lack, we feel that emptiness, and we try to fill it, we go around looking at everything, and yet nothing satisfies."

"But that's not to say that there's no place for romantic love." He knew that for certainty. There was just something fundamental inside of him that wanted to sit on a bench with the pretty girl beside him, sweet and kind, considerate and attuned to him. The way she was always looking for ways to make his life easier had struck a chord in him. And it wasn't the needy kind of chord, it was a basic, human nature thing where he wanted to get together and make them a family.

Maybe he'd always longed for that, and that's why his dad's leaving had been so difficult.

"I agree. There definitely is a place for romantic love. God made us male and female, and He intended for us to get together. Jesus confirms that in the New Testament."

"I feel like I need to be reading up, because you're miles ahead of me. Although, I do kind of know what you're talking about. Isn't that where he said that Moses allowed divorce out of the hardness of our hearts or something?"

"Yeah. I think that, and maybe marriage to multiple women. It just never worked out well anytime you see that in the Bible. I've definitely seen non-Christians using that as something that they can point to to say that Christians are hypocrites, but Jesus clearly says it was the human sinful nature that caused that type of thing to be done."

"We can blame a lot on the human sinful nature."

"Your dad's leaving."

"Sure."

He let out a sigh. He hadn't realized the anger that he harbored against his dad. He supposed even now, while he didn't feel quite so angry, he really didn't want to have a whole lot to do with him. Not that he wanted his dad to go to hell or anything, but he just...didn't really want to hang out with a man who thought it was okay to leave his wife and son. While he wanted to spend as much time as he possibly could with his mother, the kind of woman who may have raised a child that wasn't hers, that her husband had fathered with another woman during her marriage, and he'd never had a clue.

She loved him like he was her own. Of course he would admire and respect and want to spend time with someone like that.

He wasn't sure exactly where the line between right and wrong was. How much he had to do in order to show forgiveness to his dad, whether he actually had to hang out with him, to prove that he had been forgiven. He didn't know.

He just knew that he didn't want to be that kind of person. Not to his wife, if he ever got married, and not to any of his children.

"Do you want to go back to Chicago?" he asked, knowing that it was getting late and they should walk home, but he wanted to continue to talk to her.

"Is it terrible that I don't? I guess I'd like to have my driver's license back, and my bank cards, even though there wasn't really anything in them, although there will be. Just... I need to start over. I feel a little bit like I'm in limbo since I don't have those things that anchor me and make it so that I can do whatever I want. You know?"

"Yeah. I should have been on that right away. You're welcome to use my computer to get online and get a new driver's license if you want, or a new Social Security card. I'm not sure how to do that." He hesitated. "If you want to wait until tomorrow evening, I'll bring my laptop down and we can work on that together."

"I'd appreciate it. I know that I was able to give you the information you needed in order to get me signed up for payroll, but I don't know for sure that Jeff isn't using my money, you know? I mean, we didn't have joint accounts, and he didn't have access to mine, but that doesn't mean that he didn't con someone into giving him access."

"I hadn't considered that. We should get you some new cards right away so that you can open up an account. The closest place would be Blueberry Beach."

It made him feel good that she wasn't longing for Chicago. He wanted to press her further, ask her if she was planning on staying, ask her what he could do to make her want to stay, ask her…how she felt about being in a relationship with him, but it felt like too much for her. He needed to give her a little grace, remember that she had just been through two traumatic life events, not just one.

"I don't really want to, but it's probably a good idea to head back. We don't want to keep Vera there so long that she doesn't want to come back."

"True," she said with a little laugh. "Although, she could have sent us an SOS, and she didn't, so I assume that the baby is not crying and your mother is being her normal, sweet self."

"You know as I was saying that, I was thinking about the fact that she has had those belligerent episodes, that are totally out of character for her. As in, I've never seen her like that before in my life, but I guess it just goes to show that everyone has a sinful nature. She was doing a really good job of living in Christ and not allowing her sinful nature to dominate her personality, even to the point where I didn't even realize she had one. So, I guess what I'm saying is, I knew it was there, I just had never seen it."

"I understand what you're saying. She's sweet and kind, even though she isn't always in her right mind, but when she isn't sweet and kind, she's probably doing what she maybe felt like doing at times but never allowed herself to do."

"Yes. Thank you for putting into words what I was trying to say but just couldn't figure out how."

She laughed. "Sometimes it's just hard to find words."

They stood up, the fountain still bubbling softly in the background. He noticed a little girl walking along the edge of the garden and watching Skyler and him as they walked through.

"Good evening," he said as she stared at them approaching the gate.

"Hey there, sweetie," Skyler said softly.

"Hey," the girl said when she finally turned her eyes to Skyler. "I didn't want to interrupt you guys, but...Mom's gone again."

"Oh. I'm sorry, Sabrina." Skyler looked up at him and bit her lip.

He thought he might know what she wanted.

"Were you going to offer her a place to stay?" he asked softly.

He was rewarded with a smile.

"Yes. I think I have an idea for Sabrina, but she needs a safe place."

The little girl looked like she was about twelve, and while she could probably overhear what they were saying, they spoke in low tones, so maybe with the bubbling of the water, she couldn't.

"Would you like to stay with us tonight?" Skyler asked.

Sabrina's eyes lit up. "Really?"

"Sure. There are lots of spare bedrooms, and maybe you can help me cook breakfast in the morning."

"I'd like that! I've been wondering what in the world I'm going to do all summer when school's out. There's only another week or two left. I...get bored sitting at home watching TV all the time. My mom never wants to do anything when she's off work. And now that Gram... Well, anyway, I'm on my own."

"You're not on your own. You have us, and you might have somewhere else, but I need to check and see."

Homer made a note to ask Skyler what in the world she was talking about. He hadn't known that she was making plans with a little girl who sounded like she was practically homeless.

Interesting the things that happened when he was working. Maybe he should keep his window open more often. More than likely, Skyler had met this little girl in the garden.

They walked home together, Skyler between the two of them, holding his hand on one side and the little girl's hand on the other.

Homer wasn't quite sure why that made him so happy, but it did.

Twenty-One

There weren't too many times in his life where Homer had an issue that he didn't think he could fix, but this was one of them.

Not fix, figure out.

He had no idea what he was going to do. So, it was uncommon for him to take a walk in the middle of the day, but that's exactly what he did, midmorning, three days after he and Skyler had taken their evening walk.

He had spent time with her in the evening, doing what he said he would do, helping her get her Social Security card and driver's license reissued and sent to their address. They'd also been able to get online and check her bank accounts, which had not been used.

She ordered cards for that and changed her address, and they should be there within the next week. He felt like she was getting more independent, and he figured that he should have thought about that earlier, but he supposed with her having the baby and them adjusting to the new work schedule, and with his mother's issues thrown into the mix, it was understandable that they hadn't gotten to things any sooner than what they had.

But that wasn't his problem.

He walked toward the healing garden, just because Lake Michigan always seemed to draw him anytime he was outside. His mother enjoyed working in the garden, and he helped her more than once, but his favorite thing to do outside was to look at the lake. Always changing, always immense, always reminding him of how big God was and how small he was in comparison, it was something he never got tired of looking at.

As he walked closer to the healing garden, he could see a man working inside of it. Doing something to the fence, maybe adding a little more or fixing a weak spot, Homer wasn't sure. As he walked closer, he recognized his friend, Dominic. The husband of the husband-and-wife team who had put the garden in last year.

Dominic and Vera didn't spend all their time in Raspberry Ridge, but they had done a lot for the community, and Homer had agreed to supply the electricity for the garden, but Dominic and Vera had done so much more than he'd realized, and he needed to thank the man and tell him how much they enjoyed it.

Which made him realize just exactly how much time he spent inside, working. Caring for his mom. And what a blessing it was to have Skyler so he didn't have to worry about stepping outside for a few minutes to clear his head.

"It's a beautiful morning," Homer said in greeting as he stood on the other side of the fence from where the man was working.

Dominic hadn't heard him approach apparently, and his head jerked up in surprise.

"Sure is. This time of year is just gorgeous. And there's no better place to be than beside Lake Michigan."

"I have to agree with that. I... I've never been able to thank you for all the pleasure we've had from this garden, and when I saw you working, I thought this was a good time."

His friend stopped working, his hand on the fence. It was calloused and work worn, and brown from days or years in the sun. His grip was firm, and his gaze was steady and sure as it met Homer's.

"It was a labor of love."

"What a wonderful tribute for your son."

"Yeah. A memorial to him. It was also something we needed to do for our marriage. I'm not sure we would still be together if it weren't for this garden, so it's healing in more ways than one."

He wasn't used to men being so direct, especially about relationship things.

Maybe that, and the fact that he considered Dominic a friend, is what prompted him to ask his next question.

"How did it help your relationship?"

Dominic smiled a little, as though in a self-effacing way, as though he was a little embarrassed about his answer.

"It made me see that I hadn't been putting everything into my marriage that I should have been. I...took advantage of my wife. Didn't talk to her like I should. You know, when you're dating, you have a tendency to tell each other everything, and then you get married, and you know what's going to upset them, what's going to set them off, what's going to be something that they really don't want to hear, and you start keeping things from them. You don't talk about your day, because you don't want them to be upset."

He lifted his shoulder, big and muscular. "But I'm not saying that it's okay for the other side... You know, the woman's side, for them to be upset. Or worried, I mean, they shouldn't have a reaction that is so big and so scary that it makes their husband afraid to talk to them. But that's not my area. That...is theirs. I just knew in my area, I wasn't doing what I needed to do. And as we came together, working on this garden for our son, we realized there were a lot of things that either we hadn't talked about, or maybe that we didn't even know about each other. And I realized that even though there were things we didn't like about each other, there were reasons that we fell in love."

He laughed. "You can't expect those falling in love feelings to stick around. They wear off eventually, and then you're left with the normal, everyday feelings. But if you build a foundation, if you have something strong underneath, you can find that again. Even though maybe you've walked down a couple of trails that you wish you wouldn't have."

Homer didn't say anything for a little bit. That wasn't his problem at all. Although maybe the idea of building a strong foundation so that if he and Skyler ever walked down the wrong trail as the man said, they'd be able to find their way back. That's if Skyler wanted to have anything to do with him. For the long haul. But it wasn't really what he needed advice about today.

"How did you know that she was the one?" he asked, feeling a little silly to do it. It sounded like a question that a girls magazine editor might ask the latest teenage heartthrob or something.

Dominic tilted his head and ran his hand over the top of the fence. "Sometimes God has someone cross your path that you feel like you'd like to know better. I know feelings aren't the best things to make decisions on, but Vera had the same values and morals that I did. We had some things in common, she designs gardens, I build them as a landscaper. But I guess I just prayed about it after I met her, and it felt like the Lord confirmed it. And she felt that way too."

"Sounds like you two have quite a story," Homer said, thinking that maybe he could talk to Skyler about that. It didn't seem like the most romantic thing to ever say, but maybe romance was better utilized after marriage. Which was a novel idea, and he wasn't even sure where it came from.

"Yeah. I think everybody has a story. Obviously, there's some kind of story. We just sometimes don't realize that we get to choose how it goes. You know, God is the great orchestrator, and there are things that happen that we don't have any control over, but our choices determine how our life turns out. And He gives us that free choice. Mostly because He wants us to choose Him."

Homer nodded. He couldn't agree more. And sometimes he wasn't aware of the fact that every day he made choices, little and big, that affected his life moving forward.

He said a few more words, and then Homer wandered off, toward the bluffs. The town of Raspberry Ridge had never put railing up at the edge of the bluffs, there were just a couple of signs that said to proceed at your own risk and to be careful as there were cliffs ahead.

Homer stood back, not too close to the edge, and let the wind blow across his face while he enjoyed the view.

He had a choice to make today. A choice of how to proceed, and he didn't have the slightest idea of how to do that.

He had ordered clothes for Skyler, and they had arrived. He had paid extra for fast shipping, because he felt like it was important that she got them quickly. He also felt bad that he hadn't noticed that she didn't have any for so long. How blind could a man be?

But now, he didn't know how to go about giving them to her. He... didn't want her to feel beholden to him. And he didn't want her to feel like she had to like them or even keep them. He kind of thought that she wouldn't want to hurt his feelings by sending anything back. Or by giving it away.

Lord, what do I do?

The wind blew, slipping through his hair, making him wish that Skyler was with him. It might be a little bit too windy for Saylor, but she would enjoy it when she got older, although they would have to keep a good eye on her. It was a dangerous place to be with small children if one wasn't watching them closely.

As he was standing there, Dominic's words came back to him. He had to learn to be honest with Skyler and not worry about her reaction. Because her reaction wasn't something that he could control.

Maybe that didn't apply here. Maybe he just had to be honest and say he wanted to do something nice for her, so he bought her clothes. And maybe he should have asked her what she wanted, and maybe he should have given her a budget, but he was afraid she wouldn't use it.

He stood there thinking about the things he could say, and then he shook his head at himself. It seemed so easy and straightforward now. Where it had been so convoluted and difficult just a few minutes before. But the reminder that honesty is always the best policy seemed like exactly what he needed to hear about this.

How could he have thought that doing anything less was a good idea?

He had even considered giving the clothes to his mother and asking her to give them to Skyler. Of course, his mom might have forgotten all about the clothes by the next time she saw Skyler, and she might put them somewhere and forget where she put them.

He was such a foolish man sometimes.

While he was at it, maybe honesty was the best policy for moving forward in their relationship. Just like Dominic said, he could say something to Skyler and ask her how she felt. Ask her what she thought the Lord wanted her to do. Tell her that he was willing to wait, that he wasn't trying to push her, but that he really wanted to have things settled. He wanted to know for sure what she thought. He wanted to not worry that she was going to pack up and leave.

But that might have been baggage from his dad. After all, his dad had left him, and maybe that had left scars that he didn't even realize were there. Scars that would be easily opened, were someone else to walk out. It would be painful, and maybe he was just trying to avoid pain.

He took one last look at the lake and turned around, determined that he would say something to Skyler. Maybe not the second he walked into the house. She was working, and he was supposed to be. Maybe he could ask Miss Vera to come again. He didn't want to wear out her willingness to come, and he didn't want to overuse her, but he did want to have some time to talk to Skyler. Maybe he should wait until his mother and Saylor went to bed. That might be the best idea.

He started walking back down the path from the bluffs, along the trail, his heart feeling a million times lighter than it had on his way out. It was amazing how spending a little bit of time in God's creation, allowing the Lord to work in his heart and even use another person to give him the advice that he needed, could make his life seem so much easier.

He waved to Dominic on his way back through, and the man nodded and smiled at him.

Definitely Homer had spent too much time inside working. He needed to get out and mingle with the people of Raspberry Ridge. It was a nice, wholesome community. A good place to raise a family.

Twenty-Two

"How do you feel about taking a walk today?" Skyler said to Gertie as she sat at the dining room table with pieces of fabric in front of her.

She used to be an avid quilter, and while Skyler suspected she had lost the ability to do as much as she used to, she still loved going through the fabrics, running her hands over them, and sorting them into piles of oddly matched colors that made sense to only Gertie in some odd way.

"Is it raining?" Gertie asked, looking out the window.

It had been a very rainy spring, and since she had kept Sabrina overnight three nights ago, the rain hadn't let up enough for her and Gertie and Saylor to go for a walk.

Sabrina had stayed one other night, and had come home from school and spent an evening with them before going home.

Skyler wanted to ask if her mom even cared where she was, since it didn't seem like she did. She had suggested they say something to her when Sabrina was going to stay overnight, and Sabrina just shrugged her shoulders and said her mom wouldn't notice.

Skyler had insisted on getting Sabrina's mom's phone number and calling anyway, but it turned out that Sabrina was right. Or at least, her mother didn't answer the phone, and Skyler left a message, letting her know where Sabrina was, then giving her the number in case she needed to call. She never did.

She felt terrible for Sabrina, because it obviously made her feel bad that her mom didn't care. But she wasn't trying to hide it or pretend that she did. The only thing she asked was that Skyler not call the authorities.

She had said that quietly from bed after Skyler had tucked her in the first night.

Skyler's heart had gone out to her, and while she felt like maybe the authorities really should be alerted, she had told Sabrina that she wouldn't, unless she felt it was absolutely necessary, like someone's life was in danger.

At the same time, it wasn't going to stop her from trying to find someplace where Sabrina would be loved and included.

She had heard from Gertie at one point, of a homesteading family that lived not far out of Raspberry Ridge. Next to Bob and Sally.

She thought that the homesteading family might appreciate an extra set of hands, and for some reason, she thought that it might be good for Sabrina to be around other kids her age. The homesteading family also homeschooled their five children, according to Gertie anyway.

Sometimes Gertie's information wasn't exactly reliable, but Skyler intended to go ask Fran about it. If anyone in town would have the details, it would be Fran. And if it was possible to walk to their farm, ranch, or homestead, whatever it was, Skyler intended to do that with Gertie and Saylor, and see if they might be interested in helping Sabrina.

Not that Sabrina couldn't stay with her, she just... It wasn't her house. And although she had felt sure that Homer would allow Sabrina to stay, she didn't want to impose upon his hospitality, which already included her and her daughter dropping in unexpectedly and staying for the long term.

Giving Homer credit, she had to admit that the man had not batted an eye when Sabrina had stayed two nights, and maybe he would be okay if she went ahead and just...took her under her wing, but she felt that it might be better for her to do this first.

She felt like she'd settled in, and Homer, who had been working extra hours on a difficult project, seemed to like her.

But since they'd taken their walk, he hadn't really said anything.

"It's been clear for a while. I thought it would be good for us to get out in the sunshine and fresh air, and Saylor could really use a nice little walk," Skyler said, hoping Gertie would take her up on it. She sometimes took a nap in the afternoon, and Skyler could leave her, pretty confident that she wouldn't do anything she shouldn't, but she hated to since it technically was her job to stay and watch.

She bundled Saylor up and carried her out, holding the door for Gertie, who was still steady on her feet but wobbled at the oddest times, almost as though her mind wandered and she didn't pay attention to where she was walking.

Thanking Homer in her mind once again for the umbrella stroller, she tucked Saylor in, and they started off down the street

"Where are we going again?" Gertie said when they'd been walking for a couple of minutes.

"We were going to stop at the store and talk to Fran. And then, we might go to the homestead outside of town."

"Oh. Okay. It's a nice day for a walk," Gertie said like they had already talked about that.

Skyler didn't mind. Gertie was sweet and typically didn't give her any problems at all. Plus, she had a feeling that if they had been closer in age, she and Gertie would have been good friends. At least... She hoped so. Gertie was a lot different than Kylie. But Skyler realized that she was a lot different than the person she was when she was friends with Kylie. All of the books that she'd been reading had been changing her in a way that she really liked.

She supposed Jesus did that to people, if they let him. The problem was, most people didn't see anything wrong with themselves and didn't particularly care for Jesus to change anything.

The bells jingled just the way she remembered as she opened the door of Fran's store. A happy little tune that made her heart smile and was such a fun and happy welcome that she had to smile.

It was a bit of a struggle to get the stroller in, and the aisles were pretty close together. If Saylor had been at the age where she wanted to touch things, it would be difficult to push her up the aisle. As it was,

Gertie walked directly to the fabric section of the store and stood touching the material and looking at it closely.

Fran looked up from where she stood behind the counter.

"Skyler!" she said, and she sounded pleased. "It looks like you guys are out and about for a walk on this beautiful day."

"Yeah, we're enjoying the sunshine after all the rain, which I know we need, so I'm not complaining, but it's nice to have a day where the sun just makes you want to smile."

"That's exactly right. Rainy days are good, but sunny days are better."

Skyler glanced over at Gertie who was doing just fine, and then she lowered her voice. "I heard there is a homesteading family not far from here. They have five children, and they homeschool?"

Fran smiled. "You're talking about the Brandstetters. And yes, they're not far at all from here. In fact, on a nice day like today, you could walk there easily."

"I was thinking about going and visiting. Do you think that would be okay?" Skyler asked, relieved that Fran had heard of them.

"I think Mrs. Brandstetter would love to have some company. She has five boys and of course her husband. As the only lady out there on that place, she does a pile of work. And I'm sure she would like to have some female companionship."

"That's perfect. Maybe we'll walk out."

"I think that would be good for Gertie. There might have been a time, once upon a time, when she grew a lot of vegetables and was very generous at giving them to anyone in the town. The flower garden that she has now, that…is more grown over and looks like a weed garden, used to produce bountiful amounts of vegetables in season. She was quite the gardener, and she probably could have been a homesteader herself, but she was married to a surgeon and a philandering one at that." Fran's lips turned down, and Skyler almost asked what had gone on. But…it felt too much like gossip. But then again, Gertie had told her some of the details.

Still, she had determined to go to Karen and ask Karen since Gertie never mentioned Fran in their friend group. She assumed that Karen would have firsthand information, while Fran's information probably was more like gossip, since it was second- or thirdhand.

At least that's what Skyler said to herself as she bid Fran a good day and gently led Gertie back out into the sunshine.

Saylor would go for two to three hours between feedings, and Skyler was never sure when she was out whether she'd be able to find a place to nurse, so she glanced at her watch and almost decided to skip the walk for today, but then, deciding that surely a woman who had five children and was a homesteader would understand if she needed to excuse herself to nurse, she checked with Gertie to make sure she was up for a little bit of a walk and then walked up the street to where Fran had said their driveway came out on the road.

It was there, just like she said, although Skyler hadn't noticed it before.

Of course, she didn't come this way very often, typically going the opposite direction toward the lake. Somehow the lake pulled her every time she got out of the house.

White flowers bloomed along the road, washed and looking fresh from the recent rains, and the driveway, while not paved, was not muddy.

Although it was a little bit hard to push the stroller on the stones, Skyler appreciated the opportunity to exercise a bit, since she found herself sitting around the house more than she used to, whether it was holding the baby, rocking the baby, or making meals or cleaning them up.

Waitressing was a hard, physical job, and she felt a little bit like she was getting soft.

"Look at those flowers, whoever lives here knows how to raise them," Gertie said from beside her as the barn came into view around the corner. Purple and pink spring flowers grew in profusion along the edge of it.

"I saw them at the house too. She has laundry on the line and flowers in the yard. It's picture-perfect."

It looked like an old-fashioned house from the 1800s, and Skyler looked around just to make sure there were actually electric lines connected to it.

It seemed like the kind of house where they would have oil lamps and wood fireplaces.

"This is what I wanted to do, but I married a surgeon, and I ended up in town. I don't regret it. Not much of it. Except... Except the times he cheated on me."

That was the first time that Gertie had said "cheat" in relation to Phil, and Skyler wanted to stop and talk some more about it. She really wanted to know whether Homer was Gertie's child or not. Probably more than Homer wanted to know himself. He hadn't said another word about it since they talked about it a few nights ago.

They got to the house and walked up on the porch, but before she could knock, the door opened and a rosy-cheeked woman with dark hair and dark, laughing eyes looked her over from top to bottom.

"You must be serious about visiting if you took the time and effort to take that stroller up the steps. Come on in."

It was an interesting welcome and made Skyler smile and feel at home at the same time.

"Thanks," Skyler said as she followed Gertie into the house, after taking Saylor out of the stroller.

Mrs. Brandstetter introduced herself as Laura and seemed thrilled to have company. She happened to have a tea kettle on the stove and offered them tea and had them sitting at the kitchen table with mugs and sugar and cream sitting in front of them before Skyler knew what was happening. She even put a plate of cookies on the table, after looking around and saying, "We can't let the boys know I have these. Or they'll be gone in like thirty seconds."

"Where are the boys?" Gertie said, looking around as though expecting to see them popping out from behind the doorway.

"Oh, my husband has them out in the field working. It's spring and time to get the crops in. Of course, it's time to get the garden in too, and I've been mostly working on that myself, although Larry makes all the boys help for an hour when they get done working during the day. Although, everyone's tired, and no one really feels like doing much."

"So you're human after all. I wondered," Skyler said, thinking that if the lady got tired and admitted to it, then she was probably just as down to earth as she seemed.

After they chatted for a bit, Laura set her teacup down and said, "Now, I know you ladies didn't come the whole way out here just to hear me chatter on, although it's hard not to. You know I do have five boys and a husband, six males living in the house, and I don't get to do too much girl talk."

"Now that you mention it, I did have something on my mind," Skyler said slowly, as Gertie seemed to be content to sit and listen, sipping her tea once in a while and helping herself to three cookies.

"Go ahead and tell me what's on your mind. It's always good to talk to a neighbor. If I can help, you know I will."

"Well, there's this girl around town. She's been at my place several times, but for some reason, I was just thinking that maybe she might be happy around here. I had never even met you and had only heard about you from Gertie."

"Everybody knows about the homesteaders," Gertie said, as though wanting to make sure that Mrs. Brandstetter knew that they weren't gossiping about her.

"So what about this girl? What do you think I can do?" Mrs. Brandstetter asked.

"Well, she just seems bored. She loves helping me cook in the kitchen, and I know not all work is fun like that, but... I just thought maybe she'd enjoy helping around here. You know, maybe give her something productive to do. Her... Her mother doesn't seem to care too much about her and leaves her alone an awful lot. I feel bad for her, but my situation is not exactly steady."

"I was wondering about your situation. I heard some rumors, but it's always better to hear it from the horse's mouth," Mrs. Brandstetter said.

"Well, you probably heard about right if you heard that my fiancé..." She tried not to flinch when she said that word. She didn't consider Jeff her fiancé anymore. Although, she hadn't been able to tell him that she was breaking up with him, she supposed him driving away from her and leaving her stranded for more than a month was probably better than words that he wasn't interested in continuing a relationship with her.

She shook her head and tried again. "My fiancé dropped me off and drove away. That night, I went into labor, and Homer helped me. I ended up living in his house, and now Gertie and I hang out together and Saylor lives with us too, obviously."

"All right. That sounds interesting. How old is this girl?"

Skyler told her what she knew about Sabrina, and she almost felt like it was a God thing, because Mrs. Brandstetter obviously could use a girl to help around the house, and she mentioned paying her and seemed extremely interested.

Skyler promised to bring Sabrina out the next time she hung around, and they parted, with Skyler feeling very glad that she made the trip. She also felt like maybe she'd made a new friend. Mrs. Brandstetter promised to come pay her a visit and maybe even give them a little help in their garden.

All in all, Skyler was pleased and felt her visit had been profitable.

Twenty-Three

"**D**o you have a minute?"

Skyler looked up from the basket of laundry that she held. "Sure. Gertie and Saylor are both taking their afternoon naps, and I intended to slip into your office and read a little, but I wanted to fold the basket of clothes that just came out of the dryer first."

He hated to interrupt her, although his heart warmed at the thought that she had intended to come to him as soon as she was done.

"I have something to show you. Can you come?"

She nodded and followed him down the hall as he led her to his bedroom.

"I'm sorry, I have the things I want to show you in here. I... Is that okay?" He saw her pause at the door and turned and spoke.

"Sure. I just...kind of consider this your sanctuary and don't really feel like I should go in."

"You're welcome to go anywhere in the house."

Their eyes met and held, and he remembered how he felt a couple of nights before when he had sat on the bench with his arm around her, feeling safe and completely at home beside her.

It was right where he wanted to be.

"It won't take long, I just... I got a couple of things for you. And I wasn't sure how to give them to you." He gave a little shrug. "I took a little walk this morning, trying to figure it out."

"I wondered if maybe you are having a little bit of difficulty at work," she said.

He shook his head. Work was the least of his worries. "I'm sorry. I need to start out with an apology. It didn't occur to me until a few days ago that you've been wearing the same outfits every single day. I should have realized that obviously you didn't pack any clothes and didn't have anything to change into. I'm sorry about that."

"It's okay. I just have to do laundry every day. Which isn't really a hardship, and I've gotten used to it. Folding clothes is soothing in a weird way."

She gave a self-deprecating laugh, like she couldn't believe she actually enjoyed folding laundry, but she understood it. It was one of those mindless tasks that a person didn't actually have to think about in order to do, and they could use their time to think about something else. For example, a problem he was working at work or something.

"Anyway, I didn't know how to get this to you. I ordered some clothes, and they arrived yesterday, but...I didn't want you to feel like you owed me. It seems like every time I try to give you something, you think you need to pay me for it. I know that you can buy your own clothes, especially once you get your cards, but I just wanted to make sure that you had something else if you wanted."

"My goodness," she said, her hand to her throat as he handed her a couple of packages and set the rest of the packages on his bed.

"You don't have to open them here if you don't want to. I wasn't expecting you to model everything, and I'm not going to have my feelings hurt if there were things that I bought that you didn't like. I'm willing to buy you more, in fact I would like to, but I kind of thought you probably wouldn't take me up on my offer, and I just wanted to... do something nice."

"This is...way more than anything I was expecting. I don't know what to say."

"You know what? I'll make it easy for you. Don't say anything. You can stay here if you want to, you can carry the stuff over to your room.

I'm going to go back to work. Do with it whatever you want to, it's all yours."

He started to walk toward the door, but he stopped when he felt pressure on his arm and looked down to see her hand holding onto his forearm.

"Homer?"

He swallowed. He didn't know why his throat was tight and why he had so much trouble walking away from her.

"Yeah?" he finally managed to push out.

"Thank you. You've been so much better to me than I deserve, and—"

"I haven't. You deserve a lot more than what you've been given. I'm just...doing a little bit to make up for the lack."

"I don't want to have an argument right now, but thank you. Thank you for everything. Not just the clothes, but for being so kind to me. I appreciate it." He could tell that she was sincere in what she said, and he wanted to pull her close, hold her to him, press his lips to her forehead, or...something more.

He turned his feet toward the door, and her hand fell off his arm.

"I'll see you later," he said, and he walked out, smiling and loving the feeling in his chest, the one that said that he had done something and someone appreciated it, and he was happy.

Twenty-Four

Skyler couldn't stay in his room, so she carried the clothes over to hers. Not that she didn't like his room, and not that she hadn't looked around with curiosity. It was darker than hers, although the curtains were open to let the sunshine in. The colors were just...darker. There was a dark blue bedspread on his bed, and to her surprise, it had been neatly made. Maybe because he knew he was going to be taking her in to show her the clothes, she didn't know, but to give him the benefit of the doubt, she had been impressed that he had made it.

It wasn't a habit she had until after she'd moved in. She'd done it more because she didn't want to be a problem to anyone, and then she found that she liked the way her room looked after it was made. Regardless, that little detail had surprised her. That, and it was surprisingly clean. At least tidy.

She didn't look around for dust bunnies on the floor, but there were no clothes lying around and nothing else cluttering up the space. His nightstand had contained a clock and a Bible. That was it. Besides a lamp. His dresser was completely bare other than some change and a box.

She hadn't spent much time in there, and now, as she stood in front of the mirror, wearing the jeans he had bought that were a perfect fit, along with a blouse that was maybe fancier than she would normally wear, but that floated around and made her feel classy and carefree at the same time, she bit her lip, unsure what to say.

How was she going to thank him for this? And he was right, she wanted to pay him. She felt like she owed him.

These clothes were not the kind of clothes that she wore before, something she bought at the local discount store or items she picked up at the secondhand store.

These felt like expensive, classy attire that...she might buy if she were a lot richer than what she was.

Clothes that she would never be able to afford on her own.

There was a cute sundress included, which she absolutely adored, but it was too chilly out to wear. Some capris and tanks to go with them. But the outfit that she had on was her favorite. The jeans had a clean cut to them that contrasted nicely with the free flow of the shirt, and the shirt matched the color of her eyes, bringing it out and making her feel like she wasn't quite as washed out as she felt.

"What do I say?" she whispered to herself. How did she thank someone for such a gift?

And how had he managed to get all the sizes right?

She tried everything else on, and everything fit perfectly. This was the second time she'd worn this outfit, and she liked it so much she was going to keep it on.

She hadn't figured out what she was going to do when she heard Saylor fussing from the other room.

She didn't run right over, knowing that she would be fine for a bit, sometimes she would wake up and talk to herself, and she wanted to thank Homer. It wasn't something she wanted to put off.

Hearing Saylor was awake, she knew she didn't have much time. So she put the carefully folded clothes on top of her dresser. She wasn't quite sure why she didn't put them away, but she didn't and instead hurried down the hall to Homer's office.

She entered after knocking softly. He turned around with his phone pressed to his ear.

"No. I understand. Yes. That will be fine."

She pointed to her shirt and pants, mouthed "thank you," and then backed out.

He smiled at her and gave her a thumbs-up, and there was a look in his eyes that she wasn't quite sure what to make of.

Whatever it was, it made her feel warm and tingly all over. Even happier than the new clothes. Although, she was just like any other girl and loved the update to her wardrobe. Especially after wearing the baggy sweats and grimy maternity pants that she had arrived in. Along with the two oversized T-shirts.

Now that she wasn't pregnant anymore, and she was back to her prepregnancy size, it was nice to wear clothes that actually made her look good.

She hadn't even realized she was longing for that. So much had happened.

"I was looking for you," Gertie said as she came down the hall.

It sounded like she was having a lucid moment, and Skyler smiled.

"My goodness, don't you look cute."

"Thanks. I was hoping we could take a stroll around the garden before we had to come in and get supper ready. How do you feel about that?"

"I feel pretty good. It will be nice to be out in the sunshine. We've had so much rain lately."

"I need to grab Saylor. I heard her earlier, and I'll be ready to go in just a bit."

By the time she got her daughter and got downstairs, Gertie was again in a haze of the past mingling with the future, and Skyler wasn't quite sure what she did know and didn't know.

Regardless, they sat for a bit in the kitchen while Skyler nursed the baby, chatting.

Skyler's ears always pricked up when Gertie said anything about Linda or Phil or what had happened years ago, and so as they were chatting about the garden and vegetables and cooking, she was kind of letting her mind wander. Until Gertie said, "Sometimes I really had to struggle to like him."

It seemed to come out of left field, and Skyler took a moment to make sure she heard right before she said, "Like who?"

"You know, the father of your baby, Linda."

"Phil?"

"You know it was Phil. You admitted to me that you two were having an affair. I still love you both. Sometimes it hurts."

Man. Yeah, that would hurt.

"It was nice of you to give me your baby. I suppose that makes up for some things."

"Maybe."

"I should have dug a deeper hole in the garden."

"Deeper hole?" Was she planting something now? Was that all the information she was going to get today, just thanks to Linda for giving up her baby, which was something that Skyler pretty much had accepted as fact, but she knew that Homer wouldn't accept it until they heard confirmation from someone who knew.

"You know. Deep holes are always better. But sometimes when I'm by myself, I get tired, and I skim a little bit. Don't hold it against me," Gertie said with a sweet smile that Skyler figured would keep anyone from holding anything against her, except...why would she need a deep hole?

None of it made sense to Skyler, but Gertie didn't say anything more. Instead, she leaned over and cooed at the baby. "Are we ready to take a walk?"

"Yeah. Let's do that," Skyler replied, wanting to shake off the chilly feeling that had gripped hold of her backbone and felt like long fingernails squeezing into it.

But she wanted to know why. Gertie sometimes said some odd things, and it was perfectly normal for her to be talking about digging a hole in the garden, possibly to plant a tree or bush or something. There were plenty of them there. She tried to shake it off and not give it another thought as they gathered their things and went outside to stroll for a little bit.

Twenty-Five

Homer put the last screw in and stood up to look at his handiwork. It was well past midnight, and he certainly didn't need to put the rocking chair together that moment, but he wanted to. He had been so excited about it when he thought about ordering it.

He heard Skyler pacing the floor at night sometimes for hours while Saylor cried.

The crying didn't bother him, other than feeling bad that she was doing everything by herself. She should have a husband to help her. More than once, he wanted to throttle that Jeff, who didn't deserve to be running around free as a bird while Skyler did all the work for their baby.

But, if Jeff was still around, Skyler wouldn't be in Homer's house, and he wouldn't be seeming to fall more and more in love with her every day.

The Bibles had come that afternoon, and they were scheduled to get up a little early and do their Bible study together.

But if Saylor was crying a good bit overnight, he didn't expect Skyler to meet him. He wished he would have told her that, but he hadn't.

He wasn't sure where to put the rocking chair. He put it together in his study, but whether she would want it upstairs in the baby's room, or

164

downstairs where she often sat while his mom did something at the dining room table or beside her in the living room.

Maybe he should get another outdoor chair for outside. Since Skyler and Gertie spent as much time in the garden as they possibly could.

As far as he knew, Skyler had not gone to visit Karen like she wanted to. He did know she'd gone to the Brandstetters, and Sabrina hadn't been back.

He kind of missed the little girl. She was cute and maybe a little bit sassy, but she just wanted someone to love her so bad that his heart went out to her. He wished that he would have said something to Skyler about having her live with them, but it made more sense for her to be with the family who had other children.

Still, he wouldn't mind having a full house, kids running around, the noise and chaos that came with that. At least he didn't think he would. He had never experienced that, being that he was an only child.

As the baby's cries grew louder, he wondered again about the things that Skyler had said. Was he really not his mother's biological child? Why hadn't she told him? And what had prompted his own mother to give him up? That was a question he hadn't thought to ask. He'd been more interested in why his mother hadn't told him, and his cheating dad.

Kinda sounded like his dad had a history of cheating from the very beginning. If what Skyler thought was true.

When the baby's cries continued, he hesitated for a moment, and then, wondering if maybe Skyler was so exhausted that she hadn't woken up, he carefully opened the door of his study and crept down the hall.

Turning the knob in the baby's room, he cracked it open.

There were several nightlights in the room, and he could see that Skyler had heard the baby. She was walking with her, but Saylor just would not be comforted.

"Homer?" Skyler said as she turned around, looking startled.

"I'm sorry. I didn't mean to interrupt you."

She wore a T-shirt and one of the baggy sweats that she had worn for four weeks after the birth of her baby.

Why hadn't he thought to get her a nightgown?

Probably because he was a man, and nightgowns weren't on his mind.

Well, she hadn't ordered any clothes that he knew of, so maybe he could order some more including a nightgown or jammies. The first things that he had ordered had seemed to go over well, and he noticed that she wore the jeans and the blue flowing shirt he had gotten to go with it the most often.

"You're not. I'm sorry the baby woke you up."

"She didn't. I was still awake. I...have something that might help. You want to come over?"

"Over?" Skyler asked, her brows lifted, even as she gently bounced the baby and started toward the door. Like she was going to go wherever he said.

"To my office," he said.

She nodded silently, and he held the door open while she went out and padded down the hall.

He reached around her when she reached the door and opened it for her, breathing in deep and smelling the scent that was uniquely hers. Not an expensive perfume, but just clean, wholesome woman, that was more heady to him than all the expensive perfumes in the world.

"You got a rocking chair," she said in surprise. He was able to hear over the baby's crying.

"Yeah," he said, trying to keep his voice pitched low so he didn't wake his mother but also make it loud enough to be heard over Saylor's cries. "I wasn't sure where to put it, although I just got it put together tonight."

"I was going to say. It wasn't in here earlier while I was in here over naptime."

"No. The box arrived on the front porch, and I think you might have been in the kitchen. I was hoping you didn't notice, because I wanted it to be a surprise. I wasn't expecting it to be a midnight surprise, but it sounded to me like maybe we needed it tonight."

"Well, I think you should try it out first, although...not if you don't want to."

"Her cries haven't bothered me up until this point, they're not bothering me now, other than I know that they're keeping you from getting any kind of sleep, and that does bother me."

"I suppose that's motherhood."

"Motherhood wasn't meant to be done alone. You're supposed to have someone helping you."

"Sometimes what is supposed to happen doesn't," she said with a little laugh. Then she pointed to the rocking chair. "You want to try it out first?"

"I think she doesn't trust my carpentry abilities."

"Oh, I trust you just fine...but maybe you should still sit in it first," she said, and despite the late hour and her obvious exhaustion, he loved that she still had a sense of humor.

"All right. I'll sit first."

It was wide and spacious, one of the glider rocking chairs that sat low, and had wide arms along with padded backs, and was made for comfort and durability as well as ease of use.

He sat down, and she gently handed him Saylor. As she was handing Saylor off, she quit crying, like having both of them touch her was just what she wanted.

"I think she wants to be the center of attention," he said, hearing the note of laughter in his voice.

"You would think that, wouldn't you?" she said before she pulled her hands out from underneath the baby and stroked her head before straightening.

As soon as she felt her mother's touch disappear, Saylor started crying.

"I think she wants us both," Homer said, amused that Saylor was getting to the age where she could tell he was holding her and even whether there were one or two people near.

"She's going to have to choose between us, because I don't think both of us can fit on that chair."

"I think we probably could, if you don't mind sitting here," Homer said, pointing to his leg.

Honestly, when he said it, he was just thinking about the baby and helping her not to cry. He wasn't really thinking about having Skyler on his lap. But she didn't make a face or say anything else, simply turned around and settled herself gently on his leg, and that's when he was thinking that maybe it was a little more suggestive than what he intended.

Not that he minded. Not at all. In fact, she felt good and right as she settled down, and he put his arm around her so that she had some support, although she leaned into him, her head on his cheek as her hands touched the baby again.

As soon as Saylor felt both of their hands on her, she stopped crying.

"I think she might be a little spoiled," Skyler said softly.

"I think she's perfect," Homer said, and he meant that with his whole heart. Although, he wasn't sure whether he was talking about the baby or about Skyler.

The chair came with a footrest, and as Skyler snuggled deeper into his lap, he put his legs up and made sure that he had his arms safely around both girls so neither one of them would fall off.

He started thinking about how different his life was now than what it had been six weeks ago. Back then, he hadn't realized he needed anything, and now... He couldn't believe he had ever lived without them.

And that was the last thing he thought before he fell asleep.

Twenty-Six

S kyler slowly blinked. She hadn't slept so deeply in such a long time, but she came awake fast. Had she missed the baby's crying? What about Gertie?

And why did her bed feel so...odd?

Then she realized she wasn't really lying down but was still curled up on Homer's chest, her baby sleeping deeply in the crook of his other arm, while he breathed gently above her.

His breath wasn't quite as even as what she would have thought, and she wondered if he was already awake.

She moved her hand, which had been resting on his chest.

"Skyler?" His deep voice rumbled underneath her.

She wasn't sure what she was doing, just tracing the pattern of his shirt she supposed, and she made herself stop.

"I'm sorry. You must be really uncomfortable."

"My legs are asleep, and both arms too, so maybe you should take the baby before I get up, but otherwise, I had a really great night."

She lifted her head up completely that time and looked at him. He seemed like he was being honest. There was a bit of stubble on his cheeks, and his hair was a little mussed, and he looked perfectly adorable. She wanted to run her hands through it and slide them down his cheeks, but she figured she should spend most of her time being mortified instead.

Except... He said he didn't mind.

She felt his fingers move over her back politely, touching just gently but not imposing upon her. Almost as though he wanted to reassure himself with a touch that she was still okay.

It was the kind of touch she would imagine that he did over Saylor's back in the middle of the night.

Except it was the middle of the night when they had sat down there.

Dawn was just breaking, the rays of sun lightening the world outside to a deep gray.

"We were supposed to have Bible study this morning."

"I know how your night went, so if you don't make it, I understand."

"I want to. I've been looking forward to it. I... I started reading a little bit on my own, although not at the beginning, because I wanted to do that with you."

"It's good to read the Bible, with or without me. But if you still want to do Bible study, it's probably warm enough that we could do it outside on the porch."

"If Saylor wakes up, I might have to feed her first."

He opened his mouth, like he was going to say something, and she wondered if he was going to say she could bring Saylor out and she could participate in the Bible study, but... She would be bringing Saylor, but she probably wouldn't be feeding her out on the porch.

"All right," he said instead, something passing across his face so quickly she couldn't put her finger on what it was. "I'll wait for you if she wakes up."

She nodded. "I'm gonna try to get up now. Sorry, it's probably going to be a little painful for you."

"It's totally worth it," he said, and she didn't doubt for a minute that he meant that. She wasn't quite sure where they were going in their relationship, but for her, she felt totally and completely at ease.

After she was able to get up, she put her arms under Saylor, scooping her up and trying to make sure that her arms didn't drop and she didn't jerk herself awake.

She thought she might be home free, but as she pulled the baby away, one of her arms fell out, and it was enough to make her flinch and open her eyes wide.

She blinked and started to cry almost immediately.

"I guess it'll be a little bit," Skyler said, her face scrunched up in an apology.

"Perfectly fine. I understand." He looked like he'd help her if he could, but that was one thing about nursing her baby, no one could do it for her.

She smiled at the rocking chair, at the thought that Homer had put into it, to think about it, order it, and put it together, and gave him a smile before she slipped out. His eyes were steady on hers, serious, almost as though he were watching her because...he liked her. Liked what he saw.

She didn't know how he could. She was wearing the old sweats that the hospital had in their lost and found and the stained, stretched T-shirt that she'd been given as well. Her hair had to have been a huge mess, and she probably had dark circles under her eyes too, since she hadn't had a full night's sleep in more than a month.

Regardless, she went over, fed the baby, threw one of her new outfits on, and was downstairs and out on the porch thirty minutes later.

Bible study went really well. It was simply them reading together, then discussing what they read afterward, which she loved, because Homer had studied the Bible more than she had, and he had insights that she'd never thought about. She didn't really have too much to add to the conversation, but Homer didn't seem to mind. In fact, he thanked her several times after they were done and it was time for her to go in and get started on breakfast.

To her surprise, he came in and gave her a hand, cracking eggs and cooking them over easy, far better than she ever could. She couldn't flip them without breaking them, but Homer did with an ease that surprised her.

"You look like you've been doing that for years."

"I'm not really too interested in cooking, but when Mom stopped being able to, I had to learn, and eggs were an easy thing. She started with them. You really can't mess them up, unless you cook them too long when you're trying to do them like this."

"Or break them when you flip them over."

"I never really had that problem," Homer said, his eyes drawing down. "That's something you struggle with?"

"Yeah. I can't imagine doing it with the ease that you seem to. That's...a little unbelievable for me."

"Interesting," he said, like he'd never considered that it might be difficult.

It was funny the things that some people thought were easy. The same things that someone else might struggle with in a big way, but she supposed that's why God made men and women, so their strengths and weaknesses could complement each other.

They had just read about Adam and Eve being created, and Homer had said something along those lines. That men and women were different, created for different jobs, created to do different things, and God didn't intend for them to compete against each other but intended for them to complement each other. There were two genders that God created, and He created them to do different things.

Even though she knew that she naturally had the urge to care for anyone in her orbit, she hadn't thought about that as a female thing.

Even now she wasn't sure it was. Because Homer obviously cared about her. Cared for her. The rocking chair was just one thing, the clothes, the way he came over in the middle of the night to see what was wrong.

All of those things said that he cared. He just did it in a different way than she did.

Gertie came down, and they had breakfast together, a family meal that felt cozy and happy, despite the fact that neither she nor Homer had gotten much sleep the night before, and Saylor was a little fussy. After Homer left to go up to work, Skyler wanted to go for a walk.

"Saylor's fussy, and she usually calms down when she's in the stroller. Would you mind going for a walk with us, Gertie?"

"I'd love to. I like to see how my flowers are growing anyway, and getting out and being in the sunshine is good for a person's soul."

She wasn't quite sure where Gertie's mind was this morning. It seemed like it was about half there, although she wasn't quite sure.

Regardless, they walked out to the garden and strolled through, with Gertie showing her some different flowers. They settled along the edge on a bench that faced the lake, although all they could see of it from there was a little bit of water shimmering along the horizon where it met the sky.

"Did I ever tell you how I seem to be able to grow vegetables and they multiplied with ease, but I could never get pregnant myself?"

"No. I didn't know." Skyler tried to stifle a gasp. It hadn't occurred to her to wonder why Homer was an only child. But if Gertie had struggled to get pregnant, that would explain things.

"Oh, I wanted to be so bad. I really did. But sometimes the Lord just doesn't give us what we want. In fact, sometimes He leads us through troubled waters that we have no idea how we even managed to get there. But I suppose the good thing about that is, we don't have any idea how we're going to get out, either, and we have to depend on the Lord to save us. I suppose that's what happened with me."

"How so?" Skyler pretty much held her breath and prayed that Saylor would not wake up and start crying. She really wanted to hear the story.

"Well, sometimes we take matters into our own hands. And then we have regrets for the rest of our lives."

Was it Skyler's imagination, or was she staring at a certain spot in the garden? A spot that looked like it had been covered in flowers, a rectangular area that just looked a little different than the rest of the garden.

That was odd.

Skyler looked back at Gertie.

"How did you get Homer?" she dared to ask.

"I took him from Linda." Gertie gave a little smile, almost the kind of smile that someone would give if she won a competition. "She took my husband, I got her child." She paused, then nodded her head. "It wasn't a fair trade. I got the better part. Homer was such a good baby."

"What happened to Linda?"

Gertie's face jerked toward her, her eyes open wide. "We don't talk about that!" she snapped in a tone Gertie never used, then she jumped up and hobbled along the path and into the house, her steps angry and fast.

Skyler sat there, stunned. Everything in her wanted to think that Gertie had murdered Linda, which was what Gertie seemed to be inferring every time she talked about Linda disappearing, then there was that whole hole thing she talked about. But could that really be?

She just couldn't imagine Gertie murdering anyone. Killing anything. She was so sweet and gentle.

Of course, she and Homer had that whole conversation about Gertie having the same carnal thoughts as anyone else, she just did a better job of shoving them aside and living the way Christ wanted her to. Just because someone lived right didn't mean they didn't struggle with the wrong thoughts and hadn't been tempted to do the wrong actions. But surely Gertie wouldn't have acted on those thoughts.

It was time for her to pay Karen a visit. She had put it off too long.

Lunch was a little strange, since she had a lot on her mind, and she knew Homer had given her a couple of odd looks several times, but she just couldn't bring herself to tell him that she was done getting little wisps of the story, and she was going to march herself to Karen's house directly after dinner and get the lowdown on everything.

And if Karen wasn't home, so help her, she might even stop in at Fran's and get the gossip. She couldn't stand this whole feeling like the woman that she had been taking care of for the last six weeks had murdered someone in her youth.

She had called Vera and asked if she could come sit with Gertie for a couple of hours while she went to visit a friend.

Vera was not only happy to come help, but she offered to keep Saylor while she was at it.

So, Skyler nursed Saylor just before Vera was scheduled to come and then gave her a few short instructions and hurried out the door.

The sun was warm on her face, the lake breeze bracing and fresh. She felt like she was back to her old self after having a baby. Maybe she wouldn't bounce back this quickly if she was older, or if Homer hadn't taken her into his home and into his life. She owed him so much. But to be able to walk without pain wasn't something that she had given too much thought about previous to being pregnant, and being able to walk without feeling like she was carrying a fifty-pound basketball around her stomach, having no pain anywhere, and honestly, she didn't have many worries either.

It all felt rather good, she had to admit. By the time she was passing the house where Harry and Pat lived, she had convinced herself that she was being ridiculous and that Karen would straighten everything out.

"It's a beautiful day for a walk," Harry called from where he sat with his wife on the porch.

While Skyler wanted to rush past them, she figured it would be kind of rude, and she didn't want to not have time to stop and talk with the neighbors, no matter how pressing her business seemed. No one was going to die if she didn't get her answers right away.

At least she didn't think so.

So she slowed her steps and stopped at the bottom of the front porch steps. "It is, isn't it? I was just heading off to see Karen Finkle."

"Oh, then no wonder you don't have Gertie with you. Those two don't talk." Pat shook her head, like it was a sad thing.

"That's too bad. I heard they used to be rather close. And Gertie talks very highly of Karen. She enjoyed the Bible study they had together years ago."

"I'm sure she did. Those three were inseparable for a time, but you know how things happen, and people get jealous and...things turn ugly." Pat shook her head. "At one time, I wished that I could be included, and I even went a few times, but those three had such a close bond that I didn't feel comfortable. And I ended up dropping out."

"She wasn't as serious about the Bible as they were either. They were the kind of people who read the Bible and then tried to live it, too. It's... uncommon these days to find people like that. It's kind of old-fashioned too."

"It is. But I guess God doesn't change from one generation to the next. His laws are the same through time."

"They sure are. But us humans have different ways of interpreting them, and we all have a tendency to fall off the straight and narrow."

"I'm a lot more serious about the Bible than I used to be," Pat said, like she was defending herself. "I wish that I would have been more strict with my children growing up, but I kind of bought into all the things our culture told me, and I definitely regret it."

"What she's trying to say is we have two grandchildren who aren't sure whether they're boys or girls."

Tears sprang into Pat's eyes. "It's been heartbreaking, and it's torn our family apart."

Skyler didn't know what to say. She supposed that was a matter of sowing the wind and reaping the whirlwind. Once a person started saying that they didn't believe something or another in the Bible, then it kind of made the whole Bible lose its authority. Either a person believed it all, or they didn't believe any of it, because there was no place in the Bible that said that only part of it was the truth.

She hadn't quite thought about it that much, but it made sense to her now. She determined that she would make sure that Saylor understood that the Bible was the final authority. Although she supposed it was more important for her to live it than to preach it.

That was going to be hard.

For a little bit, it took her mind off thinking about Gertie and what might have happened.

"I can pray for you. But I don't have any words of wisdom. I wish I did."

"I wish I did too. It's crazy. When I went to school, biology said you were either a boy or a girl because you had an X chromosome or Y chromosome, there wasn't any of this wishy-washy nonsense like there is now. And I'm not sure that the chromosomes change just because you decide to change your gender."

"I don't know anything about it. But society changes, science changes, what's good with science today will be wrong tomorrow. Same thing for psychology. Today, the hot topics are one thing; tomorrow, they'll be something else. The thing is though, the Bible doesn't change. Neither does God. So, we can plant ourselves in the unchanging word of the Lord, or we can throw in with the shifting winds of society, science, psychology, whatever. I guess I would rather just be anchored firmly on the Lord. It doesn't really take a whole lot of brains to look at the past and figure out that whatever science tells us today, it's going to decide something else tomorrow. Whatever psychology tells us today, they're going to say something else tomorrow. But with the Bible, nothing is new. Nothing changes. It's just the same thing, all along. A handbook for humans. But we always want that new and better thing, don't we?"

She talked like a woman who had a broken heart, and Skyler did not know how to help her.

The only thing she could think to say was, "Homer and I are doing a Bible study. We just started reading the Bible through together. We're sitting on the porch at sunup. I haven't asked him if I could invite anyone to join us, but you're welcome if you want to. He knows more Bible than I realized, and he had some really good thoughts this morning."

To say the very least. He had thoughts that she was still considering, and this conversation just emphasized that. Homer had said God created them male and female. They talked about that for a little bit and the different jobs that women had versus men. Here she was, faced with the very thing that society was trying to erase.

"I'd like to come. That sounds interesting. It's not a woman-only thing, since Homer's there."

"No. You're welcome," Skyler said to Harry, encouraged that if Harry came, Pat might as well.

"I don't know if I want to get out of bed that early."

And that was the thing, Skyler thought to herself. People wanted to have the benefits of being a Christian, they wanted their children to follow the Lord, but they didn't want to give up any of their creature comforts in order to ensure that happened. Didn't want to give up sleep, didn't want to give up their early morning coffee, didn't want to give up whatever it took to put God first, to study His word. They wanted it to be easy and convenient.

Skyler knew she was the same way. If she hadn't woken up after sleeping on Homer's lap, she might not have gone to Bible study either.

Most people would say she was justified in that decision. After all, a woman with a newborn could hardly be expected to get up early when she had been up all night with her baby.

But the sacrifice of knowing God, of knowing what His Word said, studying it with others... Wasn't it worth it?

"I'm going to head out. I hope you two have a lovely afternoon. You have such a beautiful front porch." Skyler knew her words were no comfort to them, but she spoke anyway and gave them a smile.

Ultimately, their children and grandchildren were just like anyone else. They had their own will, and they could make whatever choices they wanted to.

"I'll watch for you tomorrow morning."

Twenty-Seven

S kyler stood in front of Karen Finkle's front door, swallowing down an unexpected bit of nervousness.

She was eager to talk to the woman but...a little afraid of what she might hear.

She had already knocked, and she had her hand raised to knock again, but before she could, the door opened wide.

She wasn't sure what she was expecting, but Karen looked a good bit older than Gertie, though her eyes were clear and sharp, and they gave Skyler the once-over before recognition settled inside.

"I know who you are. And I bet I know what you want."

"All right," Skyler said, not sure what kind of a greeting that was.

"You're the girl that had the baby in the garage and is staying with Homer. Supposedly to take care of Gertie."

"I am taking care of Gertie. She speaks often of you and in kind ways."

"I don't believe that for a second," Karen said.

"Well, it's true. But Gertie...doesn't always remember things very well anymore, and I have a few questions I was hoping I could ask you, if you're willing?"

She kind of hoped that Karen would at least ask her to sit down, although she wasn't necessarily expecting an invitation into her home. She certainly wasn't as welcoming as Laura had been.

But after another narrowed-eyed glance, Karen opened the door a little wider, revealing the cane that she leaned on.

"You'd better come in. This might require a cup of tea."

"Thank you. I'll never turn down a cup of tea," Skyler said pleasantly, although she hadn't drunk hot tea ever in her life before, until she'd come to Raspberry Ridge. It seemed like everybody offered it here.

Maybe it was just an old-fashioned thing, and the circles that she had run in were too busy to be bothered with tea anymore.

Regardless, she stepped in, with Karen closing the door behind her. The hall had a hardwood floor, with stairs leading up to the right, and the hall led back to the kitchen. Typical of many houses, when one came in the front door. Only Karen's house had knickknacks everywhere, shelves full of them, several interesting animal-type creatures sitting on the floor, and even a tree with lights on it sitting in the corner of the hall. If this was how cluttered the hall was, Skyler couldn't imagine the rest of the house, and indeed, the kitchen was overflowing with various pots and pans, and a mixer sat on the counter, along with a coffee-making machine and the largest microwave Skyler had ever seen.

It looked like Karen collected stuff.

"Let me clear you off a place," Karen said as she moved a few magazines and papers and notebooks aside to make room on the table for Skyler to have a spot to set her tea.

She hoped the teacup and saucer wasn't very large, since it wasn't a very big spot.

"I suppose you want to know why I did what I did to Gertie, especially since she seems like she's such a nice woman."

That was not what she had come for at all, but now that Karen mentioned it, Skyler was rather curious.

"I don't want you to tell me if you don't want to," Skyler said, which was mostly the truth. She really didn't want Karen to say anything she didn't want to say, but she wanted to hear what was going on with that, and even more things.

Karen had walked to the sink, taking the teakettle from the stove and pouring water into its spout.

"I suppose it's about time for me to come clean. I never really told too many people, but you know how these things go, you have a tendency to sweep things under the rug and continue feuding just because it feels good. Although I don't think that Gertie ever enjoyed our feud. Not like I did. But she didn't have a reason to."

"Really?" Skyler said.

"No. Gertie was just as good as and pure as you can imagine. There wasn't an ounce of guile in her. I don't know how she managed to get married to the biggest jerk this side of the Mississippi. But she did. And she adored him. Absolutely, positively adored him. She was the best wife a man could ever hope for." Karen paused after setting the teakettle on the stove and turning it on. "Therein lay the problem."

"That Gertie was perfect?" Skyler asked, wrinkling her brows. That didn't sound like the woman she thought had buried a body in her garden.

"Yeah. Because I wasn't the only one who noticed that she was perfect."

"It would have been nice if her husband would have noticed that."

"That man never noticed anything but himself, and Gertie never once said a bad word about him. Even when we knew what he did."

Maybe it was her husband who had buried the body. Maybe Gertie had helped him.

None of it was making any sense to her. Maybe it never would, with Karen seeming to talk in riddles. Or circles at least.

"What caused the rift between you and Gertie?"

"My husband, of course. He fancied himself in love with her. Propositioned her. In my house no less. At Bible study!" Karen said, making Skyler jump when her hand fell down onto the counter, making a big slap.

"Sounds like Gertie wasn't the only one married to a jerk," Skyler murmured, but Karen heard her.

"No. I suppose we all were rather lacking in our abilities to determine the character of a man. And that includes Linda, of course."

"Of course. Would you mind telling me about Linda? Gertie talks about her all the time." Gertie often got her confused with Linda, but Skyler did not mention that. She didn't want to confuse the issue.

"Linda was a flirt. She came to Bible study, and I think at first, she really meant it. Kind of like the parable of the sower and the seed where the seed falls on shallow ground, and the seed sprouts and grows at first, but then it kind of dies off. That was Linda. She was sincere about wanting to be a better Christian, and she was always a good friend, but she got distracted. Her roots did not go deep."

"Oh."

"Yeah. And of course they didn't need to, when Phil was right there. I wouldn't be the slightest bit surprised that Phil and Linda were carrying on in the house upstairs while Gertie was downstairs making them lunch. She was such a trusting soul. She never believed anything bad about anyone."

"Yeah. I can see that."

"You'd think that going through what she went through would have hardened her, but it didn't."

"What did she go through, exactly?"

"The affairs of her husband, for one. Then the fact that she couldn't get pregnant, but her husband's mistress, who happened to be one of her best friends, could."

"That's kind of what I thought. Linda got pregnant with Phil's baby. And it's Homer."

"Yeah. Linda didn't want the baby, which Gertie did not understand. I think that was probably the thing that Gertie was upset about more than anything, the fact that Linda didn't want her child. She didn't want to be bothered with the baby, didn't want the fuss and work involved. She definitely hated the fact that she was pregnant and she lost her figure. Phil lost interest the bigger she got. Which honestly, if abortions had been more convenient, Linda probably would have gone for one, but she had a guaranteed acceptance in Gertie."

"Gertie loves everyone."

"She is the most real person I've ever met. The most real Christian I've ever met. She actually lives what she believes. It's...a little bit uncanny. And I was more than a little jealous sometimes, I admit.

Which is probably why I cut contact with her so easily when my husband admitted to me that he found her attractive."

"But she wasn't interested in him?"

"No." Karen waved her hand as the teakettle started to whistle. "Nobody in their right mind would have been interested in him. He was a loser. A bum. I couldn't get him to work. All he wanted to do was sit on the couch and watch TV. I ended up working, and thankfully we only had one child to support, and by the time I realized that if our family was going to stay afloat it was going to have to be me, it was too late."

"I see. So you lost a friend and kept a no-good husband?"

"Yeah. Although looking back, I probably should have done the exact opposite, shouldn't I have?"

"They say hindsight is 20/20," Skyler said, relieved that Gertie had not killed anyone nor buried anybody in her backyard. It was funny what the mind could conjure up.

"You know though," Karen said as she poured hot water into each of their teacups, carefully holding the tea bag so the string didn't fall into the cup, "Gertie was really the one who had a lot to put up with. After what her husband did."

"Phil?"

"Yeah. Linda had the baby, and he had lost interest. He was okay with his wife raising it. I think he probably felt that it would keep her happy. He gave her a baby, she would look the other way from his indiscretions." She paused. "And that other thing."

"One other thing?"

"Well, Phil was a surgeon, a good one from what I understand. But an orthopedic surgeon. In other words, he did knee and hip and shoulder replacements on people. He didn't deliver babies."

"Of course."

"But Linda wouldn't allow anyone else to deliver her baby. She insisted that Phil be the one. And I think there was a little bit of his ego involved."

It sounded a lot like what happened with Homer and her. Homer had delivered her baby. Of course, not because he wanted to.

"Anyway, the time came for her to be delivered, and she had the baby right in Gertie's house. I don't know whether it was in Gertie's bedroom or not, because I had just found out about my husband's fascination with Gertie, and I was getting ready to cut things off with her. I was thinking I was doing it to save my marriage, but it was jealousy. Pure and simple, and easy to see looking back through thirty years of time."

"Funny how the more time passes, the clearer things can be."

"That's right. Although, I think it will always be a little fuzzy about what happened exactly with Linda. I do know that Phil wasn't the slightest bit interested in her anymore. Whether his interest would have come back after she had the baby or not, I don't know, but part of me thinks that perhaps he thought maybe he was getting rid of his problems."

"Linda died in childbirth?" Skyler wrinkled her brows. That didn't sound right. But while it didn't match up with everything Gertie had said, it matched up with a good bit. The rest could be chalked up to Gertie being confused.

"Shortly after. She had the baby just fine, but I believe she hemorrhaged. If they had been in the hospital, Phil might have been able to save her, but as it was, he wasn't able to do what needed to be done. At least, that's what he said. Whether or not he caused the hemorrhage is open to speculation. I know that's a sin, gossip and everything, but...it really did tie things up neatly for him. His wife had a baby, his mistress was gone, and as far as I know, he never made that mistake again."

"Getting a woman other than his wife pregnant?"

"Yeah. And he never got his wife pregnant, but as far as I know, there aren't any other little Phils running around. Or Phillettes."

Skyler poured milk into her tea, careful to balance it on the corner of the table, which was the only spot where there was room to set the cream down after she was done with it. Karen didn't set sugar on the table, and Skyler didn't typically use it anyway.

"Did they, by chance, bury Linda in the garden?"

"No!" Karen gave her a horrified look. "Absolutely not. I went to the funeral, but it was right after that I told Gertie I wasn't talking to her anymore. I wasn't coming to Bible study. Without Linda as a buffer between us, I knew I couldn't be kind to her. I might have admitted to her that I felt like choking her to death at times. Which…I shouldn't have said in hindsight, but we had words after the funeral. Well, I had words, Gertie was her normally sweet self, of course. Little Miss Perfect. Do you realize how hard it is to be friends with someone who's perfect?"

"I would think it would be kind of easy. After all, they would forgive you for anything and always have your back," Skyler said. Which seemed about right. She wished she had a friend who loved like Gertie did, although come to think of it, Gertie was her friend. And Gertie did love her like that.

"You're actually right. If it hadn't been for my husband, Gertie and I would still be friends. I divorced the man, but twenty years too late if you ask me. He was a worthless bum."

"You might have mentioned that," Skyler said casually as she took a sip of her hot tea.

"Yeah, well, as for your question about the garden, that's kind of odd. I didn't think about it until you mentioned it, but I'm pretty sure they buried a dog there. Phil made a lot of money, and they never had issues, but I think that the dog got pregnant, and Phil made sure that it met an early demise. Don't quote me on that, because at that time, Gertie and I weren't talking."

Skyler nodded. Maybe she was trying to hide the fact that the dog died from hunger or trying to dig a hole deep enough that animals wouldn't eat it. Maybe.

Regardless, she had pretty much found out everything she wanted to. Homer was indeed Linda's son, and Linda had died in childbirth, which made the fact that Gertie had raised Homer a little easier to swallow, although to hear Karen talk, Linda was going to give the baby to Gertie anyway.

So Homer's biological mother didn't want him, but his adoptive mother definitely did. She wasn't sure whether that would ease his mind or not.

She knew that he had hoped that he would find out that Gertie was his actual mom.

Of course, there was also the information that his dad had been a philanderer long before he was born, but he already knew that about his dad.

"You know, I guess as you get older, you get a little wiser, but I wish I wouldn't have stopped going to Bible study. I wish I wouldn't have cut things off with Gertie. I probably would have been a better person. Maybe my husband would have eventually straightened out, maybe things might have turned out differently."

"You never know, but you can't really look back and wonder. You just have to look ahead and fix what you can fix. Which, speaking of, Homer and I started a Bible study actually just this morning. We're doing it on our front porch and reading through the Bible. And then talking about it. After we read our chapters for the day. You... You're welcome to come if you'd like." Wasn't Homer going to be surprised when she went home and said they might have more than doubled attendance at their Bible study tomorrow morning?

She really didn't think he was going to mind, and in fact, she thought he would make a wonderful Bible study leader, although... would he be angry at her for thrusting that position upon him?

She didn't think so. She hadn't really seen him get angry at all. Maybe a little disconcerted, especially when he found out that his mom might not be his mom, but that would have happened to anyone. She couldn't imagine growing up thinking that someone was her mom and then finding out when she was in her thirties that it wasn't true, and her mom had never told her.

She actually had a nice chat with Karen before she finally got up to leave. She remembered what Homer had said about not staying away too long and making someone not want to come and watch his mom and the baby again.

That seemed a reasonable thing to do, and she considered it good advice. Maybe Homer had been a better influence on her than what she thought.

Regardless, she could hardly wait to go home and talk to him about what she had learned.

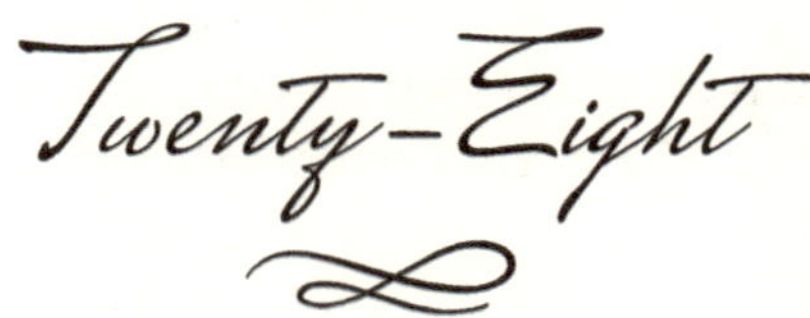

Twenty-Eight

Skyler wanted to whistle as she walked down the sidewalk toward home.

She wasn't quite sure when she'd started thinking about it as home, but she had, for sure. She didn't know how Homer would react to her news, but he wasn't the kind of man who flew off the handle over anything, and she thought that maybe he would appreciate having closure, just knowing. Since his mom wasn't able to talk about it anymore.

Unfortunately.

Again, Skyler wished that she could have been friends with Gertie when she was younger, but it had to be enough that they were friends now. It was like she told Karen, people couldn't go back, because they didn't get a do-over.

She was busy looking along the bluffs, looking at the old mansions there and the newer-looking mansion that sat on the hill. They weren't things she had focused too much on, because from Homer's house, she really couldn't see them. But here, at the other end of Raspberry Ridge, she could see those mansions clearly. Their windows gleamed in the sun, and they looked stately and classic.

She wondered about the people who lived there, although the lower one didn't look like it had anyone living in it.

Maybe she'd ask Homer, but she had so much to tell him—

Her thoughts were interrupted by a vehicle. Which wasn't completely unusual. There were few cars that passed, considering that Raspberry Ridge basically ended in a dead end at the healing garden, which had a small parking lot to the side of it where folks could go to the bluffs or follow the trail down to the lake. It wasn't a tourist hotspot, although the views were pretty, and the stone beach at the bottom of the bluffs was very nice. Or so she'd been told. In the six weeks that she'd been living there, she hadn't walked down yet.

Maybe she and Homer would do that. All of her seemed to center around him, and she got sidetracked for just a moment before she realized that the vehicle had stopped beside her.

She looked over, and it took her a full three seconds staring at the person in the truck before she realized that Jeff had come back.

"Looks like you landed on your feet," he said, and it sounded like there was a sneer in his voice. Or maybe that was the way he always talked, and she just hadn't noticed.

"Are you serious? You drove away and you left me here, and you didn't come back for six weeks, and you're complaining that I'm not what? Dead?" She hadn't realized how angry she was. She wanted to reach through the window and grab a hold of his neck.

Then, she remembered what Karen had said that she had told Gertie. About wanting to grab a hold of someone's neck and strangle them. That must have been what Gertie was talking about. Maybe Gertie had anger too. Anger toward Karen. Maybe what Karen had said had stuck with Gertie.

Most likely, Skyler would never know.

But she did know her own anger. And she also knew her anger wasn't right. They had just read in their Bible reading about Cain killing Abel. Something about his brother's blood crying out to God from the ground. She didn't want anyone's blood crying out to God because of something she had done to them.

Carefully unclutching her hands, she shoved them in her pockets.

"Hey, what can I say? I found someone else, and I got a little sidetracked."

It was only then that she realized that there was a woman sitting beside him in the truck.

In the seat where she had sat, where her purse had been when she had gotten out of the truck and he had driven away.

"I don't understand why you're back here?" Unless he was expecting to find her dead body by the side of the road and pick her bones or something.

"I want to see my kid."

"You left me. How do you even know that I had her? That she didn't die, or that I wasn't dead?"

"Carla here convinced me to come back and check. Now that I'm here, let me look at him. Does he look as handsome as his old man?" Jeff grinned, and it turned Skyler's stomach. What had she ever seen in him? After spending the last six weeks with Homer, who was kind and compassionate while still being strong and protective, she couldn't imagine spending time with that baby manchild.

Maybe she should be angry that he had someone else sitting in her seat, but she just felt a lot of pity for that girl. Poor thing didn't know what a real man was.

"Obviously I don't have a baby on me, and I don't think that you deserve to look at her or anything else. So, you can just keep on driving. I don't have anything to say to you."

She was almost home and was able to walk the twenty yards and turn the corner to go into the garden before Jeff parked the car and got out.

"Just you wait a second, missy. You don't get to dismiss me like that." He grabbed a hold of her arm and jerked her around.

"We don't have anything else to say to each other. You left, and you're gone. Keep being gone. I'm not interested in seeing you."

"Well, aren't you little Miss High-and-mighty? I thought you'd be crawling back on your hands and knees."

"That's why you brought your new girlfriend with you when you came to see how I was? After six weeks? Six weeks. I can't believe that you could just dump me somewhere and not care. Didn't you think I might have died?"

She couldn't help herself, her voice got louder, and she started to squeak.

She needed to shut her mouth and walk away. She did not have to deal with Jeff anymore.

"I figured you'd land on your feet, and I don't know why you're complaining. You sure as heck did. But then, you could always do that, couldn't you? Little Miss Sweetheart that everybody loved. You acted like a little goodie two-shoes, wouldn't sleep with someone until he put a ring on your finger. Well, how'd that work out for you?"

"You're right. That was a mistake. I wish I wouldn't have done it. Thanks for reminding me."

She had to be humble. Because it was the truth. It was a big regret, but she couldn't change the past. And she knew, knew from the book reading that she'd done, that God forgave anything. Even fornication, which is what the Bible called what she had done. But she was forgiven, which did not allow her the privilege of going back and doing the same thing again. Just because she was forgiven, and living under grace, didn't mean that she could sin whenever she wanted to.

She'd figured that out from Gertie's books as well.

Jeff narrowed his eyes at her. "You've changed. You're not the same person I knew."

"You're right. I'm not."

"But I have a right to see my baby." His tone changed, becoming more gruff, as Carla came around the corner and stood, chewing her gum and occasionally snapping it, in her cut-off top, short shorts, and flip-flops.

"I guess I don't think you do. And I'm not going to show her to you. Not now, not ever. Sorry."

Maybe she wasn't really sorry, not for not showing the baby to him. But maybe she was sorry that he wasn't a better man. That he wasn't someone who could have manned up to his responsibilities and made sure that she was okay.

"We'll see about that. I've got a right to know. I'm a dad."

"You're actually not a dad. You might be a father, but you're not a dad. And you don't have rights." She didn't think that she had put his name on the birth certificate. She had gotten all the information in the mail and set it aside. Actually, come to think of it, the nurse had filled it out.

Jeff started to say something else, but Skyler remembered she didn't have to stand there and argue with him. She supposed he could insist on a DNA test, to prove that he was the father, but then, if he wanted to do that, he would have to pay for half of her care. That would most likely be enough to convince him that he really didn't want to be a dad that bad.

Regardless, she walked in while he was still talking, yelling after her, actually, and closed the door behind her, locking it.

"My goodness, you're back fast. I thought maybe you'd be gone all afternoon."

She straightened from leaning against the door. "Really? It feels like I was gone for a really long time."

Vera walked toward her, holding a sleeping Saylor in her arms.

"Not that long. Gertie is still sleeping, and Saylor has been sleeping the whole time too. And I've just been eating up holding the baby and snuggling with her. You could have been gone for another three hours, and I would have been absolutely fine with it. It's not that often that I get to spend time with a baby anymore. And, boy, is she growing."

"Yes, she really is changing, isn't she?" Skyler looked at the cherubic face of her daughter.

"She sure is. She doesn't look like a newborn anymore."

"You're welcome to stay if you'd like."

"I probably ought to get on home. Dominic had some things he wanted to do in the garden today, and then we're going to head up to the Upper Peninsula for a while."

"I hope you guys have a good trip." It was funny, she saw Vera as her neighbor and felt a little bereft at the idea that she was going to be gone.

"Yeah. It's beautiful up there this time of year, and it has been a while since we drove over that bridge, you know the one that connects the UP to the lower part of Michigan. I love it, although only if someone else is driving."

"Maybe someday I'll get to see it. It sounds beautiful."

"Oh, I would bet that Homer is going to want to take you everywhere. Show you and that beautiful little girl off to everyone. Maybe you guys will have more children." Vera laughed a little and coolly walked to the door, saying, "I'll see you when we get back." She gave a little wave before she unlocked the door and walked out.

Maybe Jeff had gone to a different door, because Skyler didn't see him as Vera disappeared outside. She was still a little shaken up over what Vera had said, but not so shaken up that she didn't walk over to the door and lock it.

"I was just on my way down. I...heard what was going on since my window was open and you were standing in the garden."

Homer had come down the stairs, and he was standing at the end of the hall, one hand still on the banister, as he looked at her, a little uncertainly.

She cradled both arms around Saylor and hurried to Homer, who drew her like he had her hooked to a string and was reeling her in.

She didn't stop until she had leaned against his chest, putting her head underneath his chin.

His arms came around her immediately.

"I'm so glad you're here. I wasn't upset while I was talking to him, but I'm feeling the effects now, and... Vera said something."

"I heard her. She is astute. She knows exactly what I want."

"Really?" She moved her head back and looked up. "I didn't think to argue with her. I... I was so surprised when she said it, I just couldn't think of any words, and then she was gone and then...sorry." She leaned her head on his chest again, soaking in his quiet strength.

"I told you. It's what I want. It doesn't have to be what you want, but maybe someday."

"No. Seeing Jeff today, I don't understand what I ever saw in him. He's like a little boy compared to you. You are a real man. A man of character, someone who doesn't just live for yourself but has convictions, and you stick by them. You're not going to leave. You haven't left your mom, even though it was hard. Even though...she's not really your mom." She pulled her head back again and looked up, meeting his eyes when she said it and seeing the resolute expression that had landed on his face.

"I guess I knew that. Ever since we first talked about it, I realized that it was probably right. But that doesn't change the fact that Gertie is my mom. That she raised me, and she loved me just as much as any biological mom could have."

"Karen said that Linda was your mom and that she died in childbirth. Well, she hemorrhaged after you were born. Your dad delivered you."

"Interesting. Kind of the way I delivered Saylor."

"I thought that too. I mean, it's not completely similar, since..."

"Since I'm not Saylor's real dad," he finished for her.

"I guess."

"I have something I've been meaning to tell you. I thought you would say something to me when the birth certificate came, but you never did."

Her brows drew down. "I didn't even open it. I knew that I needed to keep it somewhere in a safe place, and I didn't want to lose it, and I just put it in the first drawer of my dresser. It's still there."

"We can look, but I think my name is listed on the birth certificate. I saw it when I was signing papers. The nurse had filled it out, put my name there, and you had signed, and..." He paused and swallowed. "I guess I didn't really know what I was doing, at the time, but I did have this feeling that I wanted to be a part of your life. I definitely want to be a part of it now and part of Saylor's too. And it seemed almost right somehow."

Skyler tried to process what he was saying, and she realized it didn't bother her at all. In fact, it warmed her heart beyond words to know he deliberately allowed his name to be on Saylor's birth certificate as her father. "It feels right to me for sure. I had no idea. I just signed what they told me to, and everything was so blurry."

"You've been through a lot. I understand that you might not have caught it right away. But I thought for sure you'd see it when it came, and you might even be upset with me."

"No. Never. You've been more of a dad to Saylor than Jeff ever could. You deserve whatever position you want in her life."

"Well, I'd like to be her dad, and...I guess I'd like to be your husband.

Although, I might be getting the cart ahead of the horse a little bit. I've never even kissed you."

"I don't know what you're waiting for." Skyler wasn't quite sure where those words came from, and she felt a little bold for saying them, but she was gratified when the look in Homer's eyes changed.

"Do you mean it?" he asked softly. "I was willing to wait. I thought today I was willing to wait however long it took. But I have to admit I hoped it didn't take long."

"Definitely I meant I wanted you to kiss me. I technically want to be married to you too, although I suppose you're right that it does feel a little fast."

"We've only known each other for six weeks."

"It's been a busy six weeks," she said as his head seemed to lower just a little more.

She pressed closer to him, and his hand came up, cradling the baby between them with one arm while his other arm went around her, pulling her a little more to the side, so she pressed against him while he supported the baby too.

"Is it too early for me to tell you that I love you?" he asked softly.

"I don't think so. I've been wondering for a while what this crazy feeling is every time I'm around you. When you get closer, I want to... just be with you. I think that's love. It's definitely a deeper feeling than anything I ever felt for Jeff, which I thought was love, and to my regret, I know it wasn't."

"Sometimes we're fooled."

"Until the real thing comes along, and then we see how dumb we were. I love you, Homer. I'm sure of that much anyway."

Then he lowered his head and kissed her, holding her and their daughter and making her whole world feel complete and right. She slipped her arm around him and kissed him back with her whole heart. Maybe later, she'd think about how God could take something that felt like the worst thing that ever happened to her and turn it into the best thing that ever happened to her. But for now, she'd just enjoy standing in Homer's arms, kissing him.

Twenty-Nine

Homer could stand there holding Skyler and Saylor for hours. He didn't think he'd ever get tired of having them both cuddled against his chest. He didn't realize how deeply he could love or how fiercely he would want to protect them and keep them safe.

He'd no sooner thought that than there was a hard rap at the door.

He'd forgotten about Jeff, but he should have known better than to think that a small confrontation would be the end of things. But why not? What could the man possibly want, since he'd already left Skyler high and dry, unless, of course, he'd figured out what he'd tossed aside so easily.

Skyler stiffened in his arms.

"I can handle this," he said, running a hand down over her back, loving the feel of her, but also wanting to assure her that he would not leave her to face Jeff on her own. He'd never met the man, but anyone who could leave his nine-month pregnant girlfriend with no car, no money, no phone and not come back for weeks, was not a man Homer was interested in spending much time with. Although Homer couldn't be upset with the way things had worked out, since, after all, he ended up with Jeff's girlfriend and baby.

"Do you think he's going to want to take Saylor?" There was real fear in her eyes.

He tried to look and sound as reassuring as possible.

"No. He can't. My name is on the birth certificate. He'd have to go through a lot of trouble and I don't think he's that kind of man."

"He's not." Skyler looked sad before her head lowered and she smoothed the blanket around her sleeping baby. "But..." her voice trailed off.

Another sharp rap sounded at the door.

"But what?" he asked, not moving from where he stood with his arms around her. If she didn't want him to talk to Jeff, they would just leave the door closed and ignore the knocking. There was no law that said they had to open their door anytime someone knocked.

She sighed softly and looked up at him, pleading in her gaze. "I already told you I'm so over him." She paused. "And so in love with you."

He couldn't help it. Her words made him smile so big.

"But...I know he needs Jesus." She bit her lip. "I doubt he'd be interested, but could we invite him to Bible study?"

He wanted to say no. That giving Jeff access to their life and to Saylor, especially, could end up being a very bad idea. But wasn't that what grace was? Wasn't that what God would want them to do? Wasn't that a Christian's whole purpose on earth? Not to protect themselves - they were to leave that up to the Lord and trust in Him - but to show the way for lost people to come to Christ. And if anyone was lost, Homer suspected Jeff definitely was.

"Are you sure?" he said, even though he knew she was absolutely correct with her suggestion.

"Not really. I'd rather never see him again. But God loves Jeff just as much as He loves me, and it's not right for me to act like he doesn't deserve salvation but I do."

She trembled a bit under his hands and he figured it cost her to even suggest Jeff should sit on their porch anywhere near her.

The sharp rapping came again.

"I can try to make sure nothing happens to you or Saylor, or you don't even have to go if he's there."

"He will probably say no, but I think we should offer. Maybe it will be a seed that is planted, and maybe someone will come along and water it."

He loved her big heart, her beautiful faith and her kindness to someone who had been so terrible to her.

"You know, if it weren't for Jeff being such a jerk, I might never have met you. I suppose you could say I owe him." She smiled up at him sweetly and his heart flipped over. He would do anything for her, even invite her ex-boyfriend and the father of her child to his Bible study. Which really shouldn't be such a hardship, although he found himself wanting to turn from the door and walk with Skyler and Saylor to the kitchen where they'd be safe.

Instead he dropped his hand and took a couple of steps toward the door. Skyler stayed where she was, holding the baby, as he reached the door and opened it, stepping out and closing it behind him.

He hadn't seen Jeff before, and he wasn't sure what he was expecting, but the man in front of him wasn't a terrible looking dude. He had his arm around a girl who barely looked old enough to be out of high school. The sneer on his face marred his good looks.

"I want to see my kid." It wasn't a request.

Homer clutched the door knob. He had never been in a physical altercation, but he would protect Skyler and Saylor with everything he had.

"If you want to see them, you can come to Bible study tomorrow morning at 7 am." He wasn't sure where the words came from. Maybe the Lord.

Regardless, they surprised Jeff, if his mouth opening and closing and his wide eyes were any indication.

"Bible study?" the girl beside him spit out, then she laughed.

"Yes. You're welcome too," Homer said in as calm of a voice as he could.

"As if," she said, then snorted. "I'm outta here." She spun on her heel and walked off the porch.

"My name is on the birth certificate. If you want to claim your daughter, you'll need to do it through the courts. Of course, then you'll be expected to pay for her care. I imagine a judge wouldn't look too happily on the way you abandoned Skyler. You might end up paying a little more than you'd expect because of it." Homer reminded himself to breathe and to be kind. "But you're still welcome to Bible study." He tried to smile to give his words authenticity.

Jeff swallowed. The look on his face made Homer wonder if Jeff really had figured out how much he'd lost and wanted her back.

Jeff's lips flattened and he looked to the side. "I shouldn't have left her. She...I didn't realize how much I..." His voice trailed off and the sad look disappeared from his face. "Fine. Keep the brats. Both of them. You won't be seeing me around her again. And she'd better not come running to me when you dump her. Make sure she knows that."

"It won't be necessary. My commitment is for life." He meant that with his whole soul, and he wondered how soon he could get Skyler to marry him. A month? Two?

Jeff spit before he spun and took off after the girl without another word or backward glance.

Homer didn't waste any time, but opened the door and walked back in.

"Is he gone?" Skyler asked right away, standing where he'd left her, his mother now beside her, cooing at the baby.

"Yeah. They weren't interested in Bible study, although I did invite them."

"Oh." She looked disappointed, but not devastated. "Did he threaten to come back?"

"No. When I pointed out that a judge might not take too kindly to his treatment of you and Saylor, he said you'd better not go running to him when I dump you." He paused. "Which I will never do. In fact, I was wondering how soon I can convince you to marry me. I think I'll thinking about that for a while, and see what I can come up with to convince you."

"You don't need to convince me. Just set a date."

"Tomorrow."

"Homer. A woman needs her man to pursue her. To court her. To make her feel valuable and wanted." His mom looked at him with clear eyes. He didn't want to discount her advice.

"I'll do that. I promise. For the rest of my life, I'll strive to do everything I can to pursue her and court her and let her know how much she means to me. Can't I do that after we're married?"

"Sometimes it seems like a man gets what he wants, and he doesn't feel the need to be romantic or to pursue his wife anymore. But, you're right. All of that should come after the wedding, just as much, and more, than before it."

He thought that was permission, and he wasn't going to question it. "Then all we have to do is figure out when." He looked at Skyler. She seemed to glow. Maybe it was because she saw how much he wanted her. Or maybe it was something else. But he didn't want to push her, didn't want her to make any rash decisions she would regret, but he also didn't want her to doubt or be unsure of him. He was all in for her. Completely.

His mom took the baby from Skyler before Skyler closed the distance between them and put her arms around him. He closed his eyes, knowing that it didn't matter how long they waited to get married, or in what direction their lives went, he would never get tired of holding her close to his heart.

"I love you," he murmured against the top of her head.

She responded by lifting her head and pressing her lips to his. One more thing he would never get tired of, he thought, before he stopped thinking and just kissed her back.

Thirty

Skyler walked hand-in-hand with Homer, under the rising moon which cast a romantic glow on the rippling surface of Lake Michigan. They stopped on the bluffs, the lake shimmering and shifting, as the moon stayed steady above them.

She shifted as they saw a shadow on the shore below. "Is that a man?" she asked in a soft voice, knowing that on nights like this, a voice could carry for a long distance, although the man most likely would not hear her over the crashing of the waves.

Homer shifted, putting his arm around her and drawing her closer. She went willingly. She felt a little guilty because of the relief she'd felt when Homer had told her that Jeff hadn't wanted to attend Bible study. She hadn't really wanted him to, but she'd wanted to do what Jesus would have done. Wasn't that the point of being a Christian? Maybe someday she'd be able to do right, and also have the right feelings to go along with it.

"It looks like Hobert to me."

"I don't think I've met him."

"Probably not. He lives down the shore a bit with an older gentleman whom I've always assumed to be his father, but I guess I don't know that for sure." Hobert was about Homer's age, but since the church closed, he hadn't seen him much at all. "He's a fisherman."

"Oh. Interesting. Is he married?"

Homer smiled. He wanted to be married. And the woman he wanted to marry was concerned about Hobert's marital status.

"No. But I wouldn't give up on him. After all, God dropped the perfect woman right in my lap."

"You mean, right in your garage," she said, with a teasing note in her voice.

"Maybe He was concerned I wouldn't catch you. I'm not the most athletic person in the world."

"I have every faith that you would have, and I don't care about how athletic or not you are."

He knew it. She didn't care about the areas where he lacked. She just seemed to love him the way he was. He'd never dreamed he'd have someone who didn't want to change him, but just wanted to love him.

"How about we plan a little wedding and celebration with the town in a month? I talked to Vera and Mrs. Branstetter today and they said they'd help me. I know your mom will, too, and I bet most of the town will pitch in."

"I think you're probably right." He smiled. They had a date. Even if it was a whole month away.

"I'm not sure I want to wait that long," Skyler said, as though pulling the words from his brain. "How do you feel about getting married as soon as we can, but still planning a celebration with the town?"

"I feel really, really good about that," he said, moving his eyes from the rising moon and planting them on the glowing features of his wife-to-be.

"Maybe we can make sure Hobert is invited," Skyler said. "And his dad. It's kind of sad that they live down there alone."

Homer knew all about being lonely and longing for a wife, a helpmeet, someone to walk through life with, holding her hand, making her smile, and being the one she wanted. He truly did hope that Hobert found that, too.

"Yeah, I'll go and invite him myself," he promised.

The woman in his arms smiled sweetly. "Thank you," she murmured, pressing against him as he bent his head and kissed her forehead. He couldn't imagine being more content, except he figured once they were married, he might actually feel that way. "I love you," she whispered, her words taken by the breeze and swirled around before they vanished under the soft glow of the moon.

"I love you, too. More than I could ever say." He closed his eyes and breathed deep, wanting to hold on to the moment, one of the sweetest and most precious of his life so far. But life couldn't be held. It had to be lived, and all he could do was to determine he would make the best decisions he could, and love the people in his life as hard and deep as possible. And that would be enough.

Join Jessie's list and be the first to know about new releases and sales on her books!

Read Down the Dirt Road, the next book in the Raspberry Ridge series where Amara Jardine meets a mysterious stranger on the beach and soon finds out it's her childhood enemy. Enemies to more, secret identities and family secrets are some of the tropes you'll find in this beach read. Keep reading for a sneak peek now.

Amara Jardine reached for her phone, pulling it out of her pocket as it continued to ring.

She stood on the steps of the mansion she had been raised in up until she'd been a teenager before her parents had moved the entire family to Chicago.

Memories, mostly good, but nostalgic and sad at the same time, swept through her.

She swiped her phone. "Hey, Olive. I was going to wait for you to get here before I go in."

She stood on the steps of the back porch. They never went in the front door. Guests did that. But she'd been sitting on the steps for a while, waiting for one of her other sisters to arrive. Going into this house by herself did not feel like something she was up to at the moment.

Even if she was a high-dollar marketing executive and one of the youngest in her company, at twenty-eight, to be promoted to manager of her own team.

"I'm so sorry. I got delayed again. I'm not going to make it. The flights out of Ecuador are notoriously bad, and I'm honestly not sure how soon I'll be able to get another one."

"You're still in Ecuador?" Amara said, tamping down the bit of panic that information caused her.

Her other sister, Mertie, was still at a ladies' meeting she was speaking at in Oklahoma City. Or thereabouts. It was going to be another week until Mertie made it up. The meeting was going to last three days, and then she had something else that she had to go to.

After that, Mertie said she had six weeks off, which was why Amara had taken all of her vacation as well, and the three sisters planned to spend six weeks at their parents' mansion, cleaning it out and getting it ready to put on the market.

She swallowed. "You be safe down there, okay?"

"Yeah. I'm no stranger to third world countries, but I think I'm ready to come home for a long time."

Olive had been the world traveler, and somehow she'd made it work. Amara wasn't quite sure where she got her money, although she worked wherever she went, from stewardess on airplanes to an au pair to well-off folks in Chile and South Africa.

She backpacked across the Alps and walked on the Great Wall of China.

Amara was a little jealous, but if she hadn't worked as hard as she had, she wouldn't be where she was at her job.

Not that she liked it that much. She honestly didn't, but it was a job, and it provided a paycheck and a rather luxurious way of living, and she loved the competition and the challenge.

"I'm ready to have you home for a long time." She wanted to say more. About how losing their parents had made her long to pull in and huddle with her sisters and be a family with them. It just...felt like they lost their bedrock or something, and she wanted to go back to feeling like she was still on solid ground and not have her family scattered all over the globe.

Maybe she was ready to come home.

No. She worked too hard to be where she was, and while she had worked hard to pay off her college loans, because her parents had felt that it was important for their kids to work for things, her share of the sale of her parents' condo in downtown Chicago would more than cover them.

Selling the mansion would set her up for a long time.

The idea that she wouldn't have to work had never crossed her mind, but as she sat there on the step, holding the phone to her ear and praying that her sister would get home safely, she couldn't help but think that maybe it wouldn't be a bad idea.

She could get an easy job, something with no stress to get her out of the house.

"Be safe, okay?"

"I'm always safe," Olive said easily, but it sounded like there was a new note of strain in Olive's voice as well. Maybe Olive was feeling the same kind of pressure. The pressure to...get out from underneath the pressure.

Except she'd been trotting the globe for the last ten years, surely there was no pressure in that. But maybe it was the pressure of longing for a home and family. A soft place to land. A place where people knew you and loved you anyway.

"I love you," Amara said, wishing she could hug her sister through the phone.

"Love you too. Be good, little sis." There was laughter in her voice. And it made Amara smile.

"You too."

She swiped off, and Amara sat there, looking out over the amazing view of Lake Michigan, the view she'd taken for granted when she was a little girl sleeping upstairs in her bedroom.

She hadn't been back in...years. She'd always visited her parents in their condo. And they always talked about how they should go back up to the house at Raspberry Ridge, like it wasn't a mansion, and have Christmas there or something.

But her parents, stockholders in multiple companies and on the board of multiple other companies, were way too busy to take the time to drive the whole way to Raspberry Ridge, even over Christmas.

Lots of families who were as wealthy as her parents were took extravagant vacations, but Amara's family never had. Her dad was a workaholic, and her mom worked right alongside him. There seemed to be a competition between the two of them, as to who worked the most, but she felt like there was love between them too.

She pushed the thought aside, since love hadn't happened for her, although she was only twenty-eight.

But how much longer did she want to wait? Did she want to be fifty before she finally found someone? And the guys that she dated in Chicago were...rather girlish.

She wanted a manly man. Someone who could protect her and wasn't afraid to stand up for her either.

Not someone who talked about the latest fads and fashions and TV shows.

Deciding that she could put off going into the house for a little bit longer, she stood and walked back down the steps.

She could go into the town of Raspberry Ridge. Fran's store was still there. And she heard that someone was thinking about putting a restaurant in. One of her sisters had told her that. Probably Mertie, she was the one who kept track of everything and was always on top of it all.

Amara walked down through the fields behind their mansion to the trail that met the dirt road that went down to the beach. There were a couple of old fishing docks there, and her siblings and she had hung out there a good bit when they were younger. Although they hadn't been allowed to talk to the Gilcrest boy.

She wasn't even sure where he lived. Down there somewhere, but their mother had forbidden them to speak to him. Or his family.

Which wasn't hard, since she never saw him. The area was poor and run down and difficult, though not impossible, to get to except by boat. Still, Barry Klein had his fishing boat down at the docks and scraped out a living from it somehow.

She thought he lived on his boat, if she remembered correctly. She spent hours down there, watching him mend his nets, listening to the stories of storms on the lake and more stories from back when he worked on a freighter on Lake Superior.

Those were some of the happiest memories of her childhood, and it was no wonder her feet automatically took her in that direction.

She went down the trail, which turned into a dirt road.

It didn't look well used but looked a little bigger than she remembered from childhood.

It was longer too, or she was just not used to walking, since she didn't remember it taking this long.

She was active at the gym, going three or four times a week, but maybe she needed to work on her legs more.

The lake breeze ruffled the grasses and lifted her hair off her shoulders, lifting her burdens as well, it seemed like.

She had six weeks off, six whole weeks where she didn't have to worry about her job or coworkers or what time she got up or when she went to bed at all.

She couldn't believe how freeing that felt. Although, she was also tempted to call the office and check in. After all, she worked hard to get where she was, and she didn't want to go backward by taking an entire six weeks off.

She never took days off, but her office hadn't been surprised. Since her parents had died, they knew that she would be cleaning out the mansion in Raspberry Ridge. She talked about it a good bit around the water cooler.

She hadn't needed to take off when they were cleaning out the condo, since she'd done it on the evenings and weekends, although she'd always taken work with her and tried to work and clean at the same time.

It irritated her sisters.

She closed her eyes, lifting her head and allowing the breeze to push her hair back off her shoulders, opening her eyes and allowing her gaze to fall on the pristine blue waters of the lake.

It was unbelievable how big they were, how massive, how they changed weather patterns because of their immense size, and yet she felt like she knew them intimately.

At least Lake Michigan.

It seemed different up here than it did down near Chicago, although she enjoyed walking along the lake there too.

It just wasn't the same. Wasn't this wild, wasn't as...fresh, clean, pure.

Maybe she was just romanticizing it since the lake held the memories of her childhood, back when she was young and innocent and knew exactly what she wanted out of life, and her moral compass pointed due north all the time.

She finally reached the beach area and the docks that she remembered.

It actually looked like someone had been fixing them up. The way someone had widened the road.

Interesting. It would be nice if there was a little fishing industry going on in Raspberry Ridge. It would be good for the local economy. And good for her pocketbook if she could buy fish from her hometown. That would be neat.

Feeling lighter and almost happy, she smiled when she saw what looked like Barry Klein's boat.

Someone had repainted it or refinished it, or whatever someone did to a boat, and it looked a lot less dingy than it did in her memories.

As she watched, someone came out from below the deck, walking up through the hatch and closing it behind him.

Not Barry. This was a younger man, tall and lithe, with the brown skin and ropy muscles that came from working on a boat day in and day out.

If Barry had a son, she didn't know about him. But she looked a little closer and saw that the boat was named The Berry Princess, which was the name of Barry's boat.

The man spied her as she walked down the dock, shielding her face from the sun as she looked up at him.

"This is Barry Klein's boat?" she asked, although she knew she probably should have introduced herself first.

"Used to be," the man said easily, coiling up a rope while he spoke.

"Interesting. I used to spend so much time down here, listening to his stories, watching him mend his nets and check his ropes. He would always tell me how important it was for a sailor to have good ropes."

"And to tie good knots," the man added, and she smiled.

"You knew him too?" She didn't have to say anything more. Barry always said good ropes and good knots.

"I do." The way he said it made her tilt her head to the side.

"Is he still around?"

The man nodded. "I bought his boat, but he still hangs around some. Although, he's older than the rest of us, and slower." He lifted his shoulder. "Sometimes he goes out with me, although not as often as he used to."

As he used to. It sounded like the man had owned the boat for a while.

<u>Sign up for Jessie's newsletter!</u> Get a free book, access to exclusive bonus content, get fun and funny updates on her life on the farm and more!

A Gift from Jessie

View this code through your smart phone camera to be taken to a page where you can download a FREE ebook when you sign up to get updates from Jessie Gussman! Find out why people say, "Jessie's is the only newsletter I open and read" and "You make my day brighter. Love, love, love reading your newsletters. I don't know where you find time to write books. You are so busy living life. A true blessing." and "I know from now on that I can't be drinking my morning coffee while reading your newsletter – I laughed so hard I sprayed it out all over the table!"

Claim your free book from Jessie!